BOOK CLUB AT WATTLE CREEK

Book One - Louisa Forced To Face Her Past

Alison Miles

Milestone Publishing

Copyright © 2026 Alison Miles

All rights reserved

The characters and events portrayed in this book are fictitious. Any similarity to real persons, living or dead, is coincidental and not intended by the author.

No part of this book may be reproduced, or stored in a retrieval system, or transmitted in any form or by any means, electronic, mechanical, photocopying, recording, or otherwise, without express written permission of the publisher.

Scripture quotations taken from the (NASB®) New American Standard Bible®,
Copyright © 1960, 1971, 1977, 1995, 2020 by The Lockman Foundation. Used by permission. All rights reserved.

It Is Well with My Soul

My sin—oh, the bliss of this glorious thought!
My sin, not in part but the whole,
Is nailed to the cross, and I bear it no more,
Praise the Lord, Praise the Lord, O my soul!

HORATIO G. SPAFFORD, 1873

CONTENTS

AUTHOR'S NOTE

This book is a work of fiction. However, the Hungarian and Swiss heroes mentioned—and their courageous actions—are based on real people and verifiable historical events.

The experiences of Hungarian Jews described throughout the story are drawn from general historical research. They are not based on any one individual but reflect the diverse and often tragic realities faced by Hungarian Jews during 1944–1945.

The story takes place primarily in the fictional town of Wattle Creek, set in north western New South Wales, Australia, in the year 1990. Wattle Creek, along with Louisa, her friends, and her family, are entirely fictional. Yet their spiritual journeys echo the real-life stories of countless individuals who have experienced the transforming power of Jesus Christ.

You will encounter uniquely Australian foods, birds, and animals throughout the book.

As an Australian author, I have also used Australian spelling and some unique words and expressions.

Masterfully edited by

Carla A. Thompson B.A, M.A, NBCT

PREFACE

I was prompted to write this book after reading an account of a Hungarian Holocaust survivor who eventually made his way to Australia. It was only in his later years that he revealed to his family what he had suffered during the war, and wrote a detailed account of his experiences.

He was the father of a close school friend, so I had known him since I was a child, and I corresponded briefly with him when he was in his 90s.

Although very little of his personal story appears in these pages, his testimony led me to research what happened to the Jewish people in Hungary during World War II. Some of those historical realities have been woven into this fictional narrative.

Lest we forget.

CHAPTER ONE

I live in the small town of Wattle Creek in northern New South Wales and have been extremely content here for the past year. Wattle Creek is the most delightful place I have ever lived, since escaping from the horrors of war-torn Hungary a lifetime ago.

Moving to Wattle Creek was the smartest move I could have made after the death of my soulmate. My outgoing, fun-loving Australian husband, Andrew, left me on the worst day of my life, due to a tragic accident that never should have happened. It occurred just over a year ago and had to do with a ladder, blocked guttering on our two-storey house, and me suggesting he get someone else to clear it. Neither of us was young, being both in our early 60s.

I was in our house in Sydney when I heard a yell and the unforgettable sound of a ladder crashing onto cement. I ran out to see my darling husband's body on the ground, bent at an unnatural angle. There was no blood, just stillness. I was afraid of what I would see if I went close, so I hurried inside and, with shaking hands, fumbled with the phone. I couldn't remember the emergency number, so I called our son, Michael, who lived two streets away. I don't think I made sense, but Michael arrived minutes later, having called an ambulance, not knowing what had happened. I think I said something to him like, 'Oh, Michael, Dad….' and dropped the phone.

As I didn't hang up, he told me later he could hear me breathing hard and whimpering, so he called emergency on another phone before he ran the two blocks to our home.

I was leaning against the house shaking, needing the wall

to keep me upright. Michael walked towards Andrew, bent close, then came to put his arms around me and without a word, lead me into the house.

The screaming ambulance arrived moments later.

In the days following Andrew's death, the house was filled with beloved friends and family, trying to help me cope with my nightmare.

The funeral is a blur, so I cannot recollect who was there and what was said. Andrew was a fine man and well liked everywhere he went. He was an outstanding headmaster, and I think all his staff and a large number of parents attended the funeral. Michael did the eulogy, and I was told that he talked with much pride about his father.

After Andrew's funeral, Michael drove me home, but I had no strength to walk into the cold, empty house. We sat in silence for several minutes.

'I can't do it, Michael.' He squeezed my hand, and without a word, backed out of the driveway and took me to his home.

I stayed with him and his family, and as days and nights were all shrouded in darkness, I don't know if I was there for a few days, a week or a fortnight. Sleep was impossible, so I sat in silence, surrounded by sympathetic, loving people who could find no words.

Andrew and I raised two children, Michael, who is quiet like me, and boisterous Rachael, who is like her dad. They both have families of their own and live hectic lives in Sydney.

Michael wisely called my old friend Julia and asked her to come and stay with me for a while, to help me settle in at home. He knew I couldn't be alone yet.

Julia and I had been friends since attending Bathurst Teachers' College together more than thirty years ago, and she and her husband, John, had always been 'aunty' and 'uncle' to our children. Julia and John were family to Andrew and me, even before Michael and Rachael were born. Julia had lost our dear friend John about three years before Andrew's accident, so I knew she understood my pain.

As mum and I had come to Australia from Hungary with very poor English, Julia understood my struggle in teachers' college. We became firm friends as she helped me with my studies. We even managed to teach in the same school in Sydney for many years. Several years ago, she and John moved to Wattle Creek, a little town that I had never heard of, while Andrew and I stayed in Sydney.

After Andrew's funeral, Julia sat with me as I tried to assemble the shattered remnants of my life, soon realising that staying in that house alone would be unbearable.

'I can't stay here, Julia. I can't bear to be in this house. Some things I touch were last touched by Andrew. A glimpse of his razor and toothbrush, still on the shelf in the bathroom where he left them, sent me into convulsive sobs. I am torturing myself.'

I told Julia that I needed a drastic change to survive.

Julia's eyes widened as if she had been waiting for this moment.

'Louisa, I have something to tell you, and I have been thinking a lot about this. The cute little house next to mine is for sale. It has three bedrooms, a big verandah on the front and a beautiful garden full of vegetables and flowers. I know how much you love to grow flowers. Also, there is a chicken coop and a shed and two small paddocks. You won't believe it, but it comes with three chickens and a cow. I remember you saying you missed your Hungarian cow, so I've been thinking that moving to Wattle Creek may just be the fresh start that you need. I hope you will consider it.'

She added, 'My neighbour had a family emergency and has had to move to the city to be with her daughter, who recently lost her husband. I am sad to see her leave, but she feels she has no choice but to help her daughter with the children. She is hoping someone will buy the house and love her cow and chickens as much as she has.'

Andrew and I had never visited Julia in Wattle Creek, but such a change sounded tempting, although a little frightening. I felt there would be no harm in visiting, as the change of scene would do me good. Julia had sent us pictures of the town over the years and often talked about its beauty. We had put off visiting her, despite her invitations, but now I was looking forward to seeing the town. A couple of days later, I drove the four hours to Wattle Creek with Julia to have a look for myself. As we approached the town, I became more excited, feeling that this may be the solution I needed. Seeing the open fields and contented cows reminded me of Hungary before the war.

CHAPTER TWO

What struck me first about Wattle Creek was how small it was, boasting a population of a little less than a thousand people. This sounds like a crowd, but I soon realised everyone seemed to know each other either by name or sight.

Julia gave me a tour of the town and filled me in on the local culture, which I think is typical of small towns in Australia.

Julia chuckled as she said, 'Most of the residents have lived in Wattle Creek for generations, and consider anyone who was not born here as not a 'local', even if they have lived here for over twenty years.'

When shopping with Julia, I soon learnt that there was no such thing as quickly getting groceries and heading home. There is always someone wanting to chat, or at least to wave a greeting with a smile. I was not used to such friendliness as I had never experienced it in Sydney or Budapest.

I felt eyes were on me as we entered the local coffee shop, and some customers asked Julia to introduce me. Brenda, who is the owner of the cafe, welcomed me like a long-lost friend, wrapping me in a hug. I was so shocked that I am sure she felt like she was hugging a fencepost, but her eyes still held warmth.

I am usually quiet and a bit shy, always conscious of my accent, and not willing to answer questions about my life in Hungary. I experienced no prejudice here, not so much as a raised eyebrow when I was asked where I came from.

I commented on this to Julia.

'Country people appeared to be more accepting than the city folks. No one here has looked down on me when I said I was from

Hungary. I had people in Sydney suspect I was a Nazi.'

Main Street is lined with shady trees and colourful flower pots, and runs through the centre of the town. I think every small town in Australia has a 'Main Street', which is the hub of the town's shopping and social life.

'You seem to have all the necessary facilities here, Julia.'

I counted them off on my fingers. 'You have shown me the supermarket, hospital, school, fire station, post office, bank, church, library and the chemist. I can't think what else you would need.'

Julia and I took a stroll through the beautiful park, something which is a feature in most Australian towns. Wattle Creek has a sprawling public park in the centre of the town, close to the big public swimming pool.

'I doubt if I will go near the pool, Julia, but this park is so well maintained with its old shady trees, offering protection from sun and storm and its abundance of colourful flowerbeds, that I think I would be a regular visitor.'

I could see Julia was getting excited as I was picturing myself living here.

The town is surrounded by hills and farmland, and as the name implies, there is a creek, lined with Wattle trees running along the edge of the town. The very pretty native Australian Wattles have magnificent little yellow flowers in the winter. Julia had sent me pictures of them when in full bloom, looking as though they could glow in the dark.

The creek, which flows like a river after rain, has extensive sandy shores and is popular for swimming, fishing and picnics. There is a grassy, shaded area for camping further up the creek, which is crowded in the summer. It is a very short walk from Julia's, as her house is near the edge of the town.

The house next to Julia's is prettier than she had described. There is a white picket fence at the front and a large verandah—almost the size of an extra room— looking out onto the hills in the distance. I saw myself enjoying pleasant hours sitting there.

The kitchen is bright and modern, and each room has a view of the hills, paddocks or gardens. I could not imagine a more suitable country home.

If the house wasn't enough, the gardens alone would have sold me.

They were perfectly designed for an older lady to manage. The beds were raised, so no kneeling was required. I have seen this clever idea in magazines and had wanted to have gardens like these. They were in big round metal tanks, with rocks in the bottom, Julia told me, for good drainage. There was a sprinkler in the centre of each one, raised on a pole about half a metre above the plants, so with just the turning of a tap, all the gardens would be watered. Julia's gardens were set up the same way, and she told me that she and her neighbour had them made at the same time. Her friend had left the gardens filled with flowering plants and vegetables, and Julia had been commissioned to keep them weeded and watered, ready for the new owner.

It may sound silly, but the idea of having a cow and fresh milk again was the final bit of news that made the place irresistible! There is something therapeutic about milking a contented cow— I'm sorry too few people get to experience it.

When I first met Bessie, she nudged me gently with her velvet nose and watched me with her deep brown eyes, as if to welcome me into the neighbourhood. It was love at first sight, and I could see the poor girl desperately needed milking. A local farmer had been coming by to milk her every second day, but to Julia's amazement, within minutes, I had a bucket and was perched on the three-legged milking stool in the shed, relieving her of her milk. I was a child again in happier times in Hungary.

I didn't buy the house immediately but spent the next two weeks with Julia, falling in love with the town.

The local vet, Dr Jim Samuels, came and checked Bessie to make sure she was fit before I officially took possession of her. He stayed for a cup of tea and a chat as we got to know each other. I could see he was very fond of Bessie, and I had heard good reports of him from Julia. He is well loved in Wattle Creek and considered a very fine vet. She added that people are concerned to hear he is talking of retiring and that he and his wife Judy are planning to tour Australia in their caravan.

When I called Michael and Rachael and told them I had bought the house, they were shocked. It was uncharacteristic of me to be hasty, so they were worried. They told me later that they thought perhaps grief had made me impulsive.

They arrived together the following weekend and were relieved when they saw my cute country cottage and the surrounding gardens. They were also impressed with the pretty town and its friendly inhabitants. They loved Aunty Julia and were sure it would do me good to be living near her again.

Michael has a construction company, and was quick to check that the house was structurally sound and not riddled with termites. I knew enough to have a building inspection before I signed the paperwork, but it was reassuring to have his approval.

Rachael squeezed me, saying, 'Mum, you are not just the sweetest person I know, but also the bravest. After Dad died, we thought you might never recover as you two were very happy together. And yet, you have bravely started a new life, even arranging to move to a new town, far from all that is familiar. You keep looking ahead instead of behind. I know you will miss Dad every day, as we all will, but we are confident now that you are going to be okay, because of the strong, positive person you have always been. You are such an inspiration, and I know Dad would be proud of you.'

She smiled. 'But I couldn't live here, Mum. It's too small for me, but I know you will make it work.' Rachael then added with a wink, 'It might be fun to come here for holidays.'

'You had better come,' I laughed. I hugged her tightly, forcing down the lump in my throat, thankful for her kind words. 'I will miss having you close by, Rach, so I want lots of visits.'

Michael said, 'I'm glad you are not selling the family home

yet, though. We already have people interested in renting it, so you know it will be there if you ever want to come back.'

Always practical and thoughtful is my dear Michael.

I travelled back to Sydney with my children, and they helped me pack up my belongings over the following two weeks and organise a removalist to bring my furniture up to Wattle Creek. I was moving from a big house to a little country cottage, so a large number of things were sold, or added to Michael's and Rachael's homes.

Not long after I settled into my new house, Julia held a welcome morning tea for me. I met several of the local ladies, and boisterous Brenda, from the coffee shop with the cute name 'Common Ground', was also able to join us. It is the hub of social life in the town, and Julia and I are now regular patrons. It is always alive with the chatter of happy customers, and the smell of coffee drifting into the street, is perhaps Brenda' secret weapon to draw them inside.

I was surprised that I hadn't met my neighbour on the other side of my property, as she didn't come to the morning tea. Julia hadn't told me anything about her, but said I was sure to meet her someday.

My life settled into a comfortable and enjoyable rhythm. I would milk Bessie every morning at about 6:30 and enjoyed starting every day chatting to her. I love growing flowers and vegetables, so a couple of hours each day in the garden was a pleasure.

I began regularly walking along the riverbank soon after I moved in, either in the evenings or after milking. The weather was still hot, so in the cool of the evening, it was very pleasant by the creek, as long as I was well protected from the mosquitoes. Julia had warned me, so I had plenty of repellent!

I could feel my health improving soon after I started this routine, as I had not been disciplined to make time for exercise in the city. The pollution from the crowded streets was not conducive to evening walks, and I didn't feel safe if I went alone.

I'm sure the homegrown vegetables, eggs, milk, and local meat also improved my health.

I decided to get a dog for company in the house and on my walks, so with Julia's help, I put an ad on the community notice board outside the cafe. It wasn't long before I had a call from a young man heading to the city to study. He said he had a dog and a cat that needed homes, and he was reluctant to separate them as they had grown up together. That is how I came to have Mango the ginger cat and her companion, Gypsy a golden retriever.

Rachael, Michael and their families came for a long weekend a month after I had settled in. They all commented on how much healthier I looked, saying that they were sure this new life in the country was the best move I could have made.

I shocked them when I said, 'I have started playing tennis again after all these years.'

I used to play and was pretty good when my children were young, but had not played for at least ten years.

'I have joined the tennis club and have started to play regularly with a lady called Irene, who is about my age and married to the mayor. She has lived here all her life and seems to know everyone.'

Before they headed back to the big smoke, Michael admitted, 'I have been very worried about you, Mum. I thought you may have made a big mistake moving here so far from us. I am relieved to see how happy you are and how much healthier you look already. You have made a very tough decision, but I am convinced it was the right one. Most people I know would not have the courage to make such a change.'

Julia and I waved them away on the following Monday afternoon, sad to see them leave, but with my arm around my old friend, I knew I would never feel lonely in Wattle Creek

CHAPTER THREE

I did eventually meet my neighbour, Terry, who lives in the house on the opposite side from Julia. My friend had been reluctant to talk about her, and I am not sure she was invited to the welcome morning tea. No one mentioned her or seemed surprised that she wasn't there.

Her house is a little higher than mine and looks down on my backyard. There is a small vacant block between our houses, so we are not uncomfortably close. I don't know who owns it, and Julia has never seen anyone there, except a young man who mows the grass.

When working in my back garden, I have sometimes seen a curtain move in one of Terry's windows and felt that she was watching me, so I pressed Julia for more information.

'She moved here about a year before you came, Louisa. No one knows much about her as she keeps to herself and doesn't socialise at all.'

Julia added, 'I took a welcome cake to her when she moved in, but she opened the door just a fraction to receive it. She said her name was Terry when I introduced myself, but the conversation went no further.'

Julia's cake plate was returned, stuffed into her letterbox.

'I have invited her for coffee several times, Louisa, but she always says she is too busy.'

Not usually a busybody, I caught myself watching her place and had only seen her take short outings, perhaps just for groceries or a trip to the bank or post office. I never see her in town or at the cafe. Just a recluse, I thought, and that was her choice.

The interaction I have had with her over the last year has been unpleasant. I try to be friendly when I see her, but she is always cold and distant.

She only comes onto my property to complain. For example, sometimes my rooster crows far too early and wakes her. She blames me and tells me I must do something about it. She has even suggested it would be better if I ate my dear old boy.

She complains about my cow bringing flies to her place, but the paddocks near us are home to hundreds of cows; yet she insists it is my Bessie that is the cause of the problem.

Despite her sour personality, she is very attractive. She is tall, elegant and strikingly beautiful, possibly in her late forties.

Rumour has it that she used to be a high-flying executive in Canberra before she moved here, and I heard she had also been a model.

I tried to be kind to her as I don't want to upset or offend anyone, but she wouldn't allow me to even pass the time of day with her. When she came to complain or yell over her fence, there was no opportunity for me to defend myself or my animals, as she always left before I could reply. She often complains that my TV or music are too loud, despite the fact that we have a small paddock between us. I know I am getting a little hard of hearing as I age, but Julia assures me she can never hear either from her place, and her house is a lot closer.

I have occasionally dropped some flowers or vegetables on Terry's porch, and although I know she takes them inside, my small gifts were never acknowledged. I had also offered her fresh milk, but she said raw milk is poisonous.

So, Terry had been the only small black cloud in my first year in Wattle Creek. I seem to be able to do a good job of keeping my distance, always making a conscious effort to keep down the noise, and control anything else she may find a reason for complaint.

She was a bit of a mystery, hurting but unreachable. Her presence was like a blowfly buzzing around my face which I couldn't manage to brush away. I determined to do my best to ignore her and enjoy a quiet life.

Julia and I see each other most days, for a chat over the fence or a cup of tea together. It is wonderful for me to be living this close to my old friend again.

Earlier this year, Julia dropped in for an afternoon cup of tea and a chat, with a bit of news.

'Louisa, I just heard a ladies' book club is starting and was thinking we should go together.'

My enthusiasm surprised her when I answered that I would love to go. As my first year in Wattle Creek was drawing to a close, I was learning to live with my grief, facing life without Andrew. I had been content up until this point to spend my time with Julia or alone, with no desire to make new friends. I didn't think I would ever laugh or even smile again after Andrew died, but I had recently felt my love of life returning, so I was feeling ready to try and move forward and make some friends. I have always loved books and I love people. Most people, Terry being the only exception. I had been hopeful that no one would have invited her to join the book club.

However, the day before our first book club meeting, I heard a sharp knock on my door.

Gypsy, although too friendly to be a guard dog, started a low growl whenever Terry came on my property and Mango would hide under a chair. As I opened the door, she stormed across the threshold, rolled up her sleeve and poked her skinny arm in my face.

'Look. Bites! Is it your stupid cow, your chickens or that mangy mutt of yours that is attracting the sandflies?'

Through clenched teeth, I told her to leave, and she stormed out, muttering under her breath. She was probably as shocked at my anger as I was, as I had never spoken to anyone like that. Perhaps with every unpleasant encounter, my annoyance had been nudged a little higher, like water nearing boiling point, and I was more exasperated with her than I had realised.

I was sure that no one would have invited her to join the book club, or if she was invited, she would not attend, as she didn't like anyone.

However, my heart sank when Julia and I walked through the door for the first meeting with snacks in hand and I immediately saw her sitting alone drinking coffee, looking out of place and not talking to anyone. I was determined to ignore her.

The gatherings were to be held weekly at Karen's house, as it was her idea to start the book club and she had a loungeroom spacious enough for the eight of us to fit comfortably. I had met Karen at Julia's, but I had kept my distance as I knew she was religious. I heard her husband, David, pastored the church which stood beside their cosy brick house. This was the closest I had ever been to a church, and I was sure it was the closest I would ever come.

The delightful aroma of freshly brewed coffee and homemade pie filled the air, and the soft sound of laughter created a warm, welcoming atmosphere. A variety of treats covered a large wooden coffee table occupying the centre of the room. I felt optimistic about the times that we would spend together, sharing our thoughts on various books. They seemed like a warm group of women whom I would enjoy getting to know.

None of us followed the latest fad diets, so with heaps of cream piled on top, we all devoured generous helpings of Karen's blueberry pie. I contributed the fresh cream, donated by my Bessie.

We didn't have a book to discuss in the first week, but instead used the morning to get to know each other. Someone suggested that we all share a bit about ourselves, as although most faces were familiar, we didn't all know each other well.

Karen began. 'I'm thrilled that you have all come today, and I am excited to get to know you all as we share books together. My husband David and I, and our two teenage sons have fallen in love with Wattle Creek and have enjoyed the six years we have been here.'

Warmth flowed from Karen, enveloping us all like a snug blanket on a bitter winter's night and helping everyone feel comfortable and welcome. I had never met a friendly preacher's wife before.

Each lady shared the skeleton of their story, and I expected that over the coming months, some flesh would appear on the bones.

Terry introduced herself, proudly telling us about her impressive education and the prestigious job she had held for almost twenty years until her early retirement. She said she moved to Wattle Creek, just two years ago, but she shared nothing about her family. Karen was the only one who offered her an encouraging smile.

'My name is Louisa, and I am Jewish,' I said, when it was my turn.

I don't usually mention that and didn't plan to say it. I was shocked when it rolled off my tongue, as being Jewish had caused my family more pain than I thought I would ever share. Most of the ladies smiled when I said it, which gave me the courage to continue.

'I left Hungary in my late teens and eventually came to Australia. I'm sure you have noticed my accent.'

As I used the word 'eventually', I imagined a seagull soaring effortlessly above a raging sea. I hoped all eyes were on the gull and no one caught a glimpse of the storm beneath, and would ask me about those waves.

Surely not. After all, this is a book club, not group therapy.

I convinced myself that we would all put on our smiling masks and get together to sip tea and talk about books, and I was looking forward to that. However, I was determined to keep my secrets hidden behind my smile.

I didn't miss the smirk that flashed across Terry's face when I mentioned being Jewish.

As we left the meeting, her face contorted, 'Wait 'til I tell my friends I have a Jew next door.' Her comment didn't unsettle me.

I knew she had no friends.

CHAPTER FOUR

Terry, whom I nicknamed 'Terror', continued to attend our meetings, although she did not fit in, like trying to blend water with oil. She usually remained quiet, but her occasional comments were negative. I was determined to ignore her and enjoy the time with the other ladies, expecting the meetings and the books to be enjoyable.

Our first book, *Nothing Can Divide Us*, was a light-hearted story of two best friends going on a road trip fresh out of high school. They faced challenges in their travels and also in their friendship. At one point, they argued so much about which road to take that they stopped and camped for three days without speaking to each other, as they were both stubborn. On the third day, one girl looked at her friend, and when their eyes met, they both erupted into laughter, each acknowledging how childish they had been. What followed were tears and hugs, amidst repeated apologies. They hit the road once more, determined not to allow a silly disagreement to come between them again. On the remainder of their journey, they were able to face dangers and setbacks together, as an unbreakable force against the obstacles they encountered.

We all enjoyed their adventures, but Terry assured us it was unrealistic. She said one girl would inevitably betray the other.

'A friendship like that is pure fiction. It could not survive a road trip. At some point, there would be friction and hurt, and they would go their separate ways. The smart thing is not to let anyone ever get that close to you.'

I thought, 'Don't worry, Terror. No one will make any attempt to get close to you.' I don't usually have such nasty thoughts, so I was shocked when this came to my mind. Somehow, her past year of constant complaining had worn me down, and I was not pleased to find myself thinking such an ugly thought.

Our second book, titled *Bit by Bit*, told the story of a thief who repeatedly stole small amounts from the cash register at work. It had us on the edge of our seats as she often narrowly escaped detection. We had an interesting discussion as some of us sided with the thief and hoped she wouldn't get caught, whereas others were frustrated that she managed to steal successfully. Our emotions seesawed like a child on a playground, up with compassion one moment, then down with frustration when she wasn't caught.

She used the stolen money to support her aged parents, which evoked our sympathy. When caught, the judge, instead of sending her to gaol, gave her one hundred hours of community service. His sentence was lenient because her parents would be destitute if she was incarcerated. He warned her that if she stole again, she would serve a minimum of three years in prison. We debated the fairness of the sentence, with some suggesting it was too lenient. Julia sided with the thief, telling us we didn't understand the temptation she faced.

She insisted, 'After discovering it to be easy the first few times, it would have been hard for her to stop, even if she wanted to. I don't see her as basically a bad person, but just as someone who desperately needed the money.'

The discussion interested us all, but I was confused by Julia's ardent defence of the thief. We all discussed the book lightheartedly, but Julia was passionate in her support of the girl. She seemed to be almost angry at us wanting her to be caught and suffer the full extent of the law. I didn't understand why the book bothered her so much. It seemed out of character for her to feel very passionate about a story and adamant in her defence of a thief.

The flesh started appearing on the bones of our personal stories. Some felt safe enough to share past failures, disappointments and present-day fears, as trust and friendships grew. We ranged in age from a young mother in her early 40s to a few who were closer to my age. The love of books brought us together, making age irrelevant. I was enjoying getting to know these ladies and made plans to invite them to my home one by one to deepen these new friendships.

A few weeks after our first book club meeting, an offhand remark detonated a bomb in my head, sending fiery shrapnel through my brain, making it impossible to think. This time, the revelation was so shocking, even unthinkable, that I could scarcely believe the words I had just heard. My happy, peaceful life would never be the same.

We were enjoying tea and cake while discussing our latest book, *Shock Therapy*. It was the true story of a man who received shocking news that ultimately enriched his life in unexpected ways. What at first almost destroyed him became the source of deep healing. As we read it, we all admitted to feeling that he was doomed to a life of constant misery, so we were surprised and pleased to see that the shock opened the doors for his healing and renewal.

At the close of the discussion, one of the ladies casually mentioned a man who had recently moved to our town.

'Hey, did you all meet the new owner of our supermarket? He is friendly and helpful, very much better than the grump we had before.'

She then turned to me and smiled, 'His name is Dorjan Halmi, Louisa, and he too is from Hungary. Have you met him yet? How special for you to have someone from your homeland now living here in Wattle Creek.'

It was this simple statement that caused my safe, predictable world to suddenly wobble uncontrollably on its axis, like a spinning top teetering slowly just before its fall.

I didn't realise I had spent my life walking along a balance beam. It had become effortless until someone unknowingly shook that beam.

No one saw the beam shake. No one saw me crouched over, trembling, clutching the beam, struggling to keep my balance.

My shaking hand carefully placed my teacup on its saucer, as every cell in my body snapped to attention. The mention of his name. Not a common name.

There could not be two Dorjan Halmis in this world.

My face flushed as panic engulfed me like a wave crashing over me, pushing me to the ocean floor.

I left the book club meeting as soon as possible, hoping not to attract attention. I drove home alone somehow and collapsed on my couch, curled into a ball and tried to think. But I could only cry. I thought I had left my painfilled past far behind, and now it had found me.

CHAPTER FIVE

I decided the best way to cope with the news of that man's arrival was to withdraw from the book club and hide away, feigning illness. I spent the following days wandering from room to room but doing nothing. To sit still was impossible as my mind gave me no rest. Details of my past crashed into my thoughts like a tsunami that I could not outrun. The swirling waters in my mind showed no sign of easing. I was caught in the flood and was drowning. I had no escape as the pain and despair continually washed over me. Sleep became impossible, food tasteless.

I had a past, tragic, frightening and unjust, which I was now reliving. I could not cope with what had happened to my beloved country, my fellow Jews and my own family. No one deserved the horrors we lived through. Revisiting it was unbearable. The pain that resurfaced shocked me, as I had convinced myself I had healed years ago. I heard that time heals all wounds, but I now knew I had believed a lie and that realisation led to deep despair. I expected the rest of my life to be filled with the pain of my past without any possibility of relief. The hatred I had for that monster raged fiercer than ever, as fresh as when I had endured his cruelty so long ago.

I left the house, when necessary, just to tend my garden and milk my cow. When Julia saw me in the garden, she would hurry over to the fence to talk to me, but as soon as I saw her, I would drop anything I was holding and rush inside, and bolt the door, locking my old friend out both physically and emotionally.

The ladies continued to bring their empty milk containers, leaving them on my verandah. I filled them and put them in a tub with ice to be collected. Some left messages with their milk containers, some phoned and some knocked on my door, but I didn't respond to anyone. They knew I was home, as Julia reported her sightings of me in the garden, and Bessie was being milked.

For two long weeks, my brain had been telling me to grow up, get over it, move on, and stop being a baby.

But my heart shouted back, 'You don't understand how it hurts. You don't understand what I endured. You don't understand.'

The heart-mind debate never let up, and perhaps that torment led to my physical decline. Internal wars are brutal to body, soul and spirit.

I planned to calm myself by reading the book for our next meeting, which Julia had left on my verandah. When I saw the title, *They Came for Us*, and that it described life in a European village during World War Two, I threw it across the room. I was tempted to rip it to shreds, but instead left it crumpled in a corner.

After I had endured these two foolish, miserable weeks, Julia thumped on my door, peered through my windows, calling my name. I hid, curled up on my couch, hoping she would give up and go home, but she persisted. She repeatedly rang the doorbell, which normally I was delighted to hear, but that day it was as jarring as the shriek of the dentist's drill. I was forced to eventually crack open the door, and I silently stared at her. The shell of my flimsy cocoon was crumbling despite my belief that it held firm. I had kept it intact, and nothing and no one, not even my Andrew, had broken through. The mention of one man's name caused a crack, and Julia was about to dismantle it completely. She pushed my door open, stormed in and sat, with a face that said she would not leave without an explanation.

'You look terrible, Louisa. And I'm not just talking about your clothes and hair. What has happened to you?'

I looked down at my baggy gardening jumper and dirty jeans

and shrugged.

She said I looked like I hadn't slept for days, which was true, or showered or combed my hair, which was probably also true.

My dearest friend Julia had barged into the middle of my battle, inching the door of my heart open, as I shoved against it. I felt like a mouse trying to stop a steamroller.

Sitting together on the couch, she took both my hands in hers and said, 'Dorjan Halmi.'

I flinched as if she had hit me.

'Louisa, I think you should talk about it. Please tell me what happened.'

I sighed long and heavy as the flood was unstoppable.

Julia waited for my tears to subside, and wiping water from her own eyes, she wrapped me in a warm hug. The tenderness of my friend enabled me to speak.

I took a breath and spoke that name through clenched teeth. 'Dorjan Halmi.' But I couldn't continue.

To break the silence, Julia said, 'The book club ladies are worried about you. We don't understand you shunning us all. They are not offended, Louisa, they are concerned.'

After a moment, she added, 'Come on, Louisa. I am here for you. We are old friends. You need to get it out. Talk to me. Tell me what happened.'

Amidst tears and deep sighs, I managed to sob through parts of my story.

CHAPTER SIX

I told Julia about the war in Hungary and described briefly how harshly Jews had been treated. However, talking about my family's experiences proved much harder.

'I had a brother, Julia. We were as close as twins. Asher and I were always together. His kindness and patience with me, his little sister, caused me to adore him. I always felt proud when I was with him, as he was extremely popular, and I knew I held a special place in his heart. All our friends looked up to him as he was kind to everyone, rich or poor. He was smart and hoped one day to be a doctor as he wanted to help people. You would have loved him.

'Asher joined the Fire Brigade soon after the occupation of Hungary in 1944. We thought he would be safe from being sent to a ghetto or a concentration camp.

'One day, Dorjan approached while Asher and I were enjoying a rare walk together. We both knew him, as he had attended the same school as my brother, often in the same classes. However, now he wore the uniform of the dreaded Arrow Cross Party, modelled on the Nazi Youth of Germany. I was terrified as I had heard a lot about the brutality of the members of this party, having been brainwashed into believing that Jews should not be allowed to live. They had been taught to believe that we were not fully human.

'Now that creep had become one of them. He was wearing the uniform proudly, as though it was a badge of honour. But it was a disgusting uniform, worn by hate-filled, indoctrinated young people.'

'Asher started joking and chatting with his friend, and was surprised when Dorjan started flirting with me and scaring me. He came over to me, sneering at me, stroking my face and putting his arm around me. He had a sinister look in his eyes that I had never seen before.

'Asher recognised his intentions and became angry.

'Get your hands off my sister,' he yelled, as he rushed towards me, ready to fight Dorjan if necessary.

He started swearing at Asher and called him a 'zsidó', a derogatory Hungarian word for Jew. He punched Asher in the face, knocked him to the ground with the butt of his rifle, and then started kicking him, while I stood frozen, screaming'.

'He pulled Asher to his feet, jammed his rifle into his back and through gritted teeth, commanded him to get into his armed vehicle. Dazed and bloody, Asher turned and looked at me as the heartless animal forced him to walk away. Julia, I never saw him again. The picture of his bleeding, distressed face, looking back at me, longing to protect me still, will stay with me forever.'

'Oh Louisa, that breaks my heart. How could someone treat a friend like that? What did you do? Did you rush after them?'

Julia gently stroked my back as I cried, reliving those terrible moments for more than the thousandth time. She waited patiently for me to continue, while she was imagining the horror of those minutes.

At last, I whispered, 'People nearby hurried away, for fear of what may happen to them. I stood alone, unable to move or speak. A kind neighbour found me, and placing her arms around me, slowly walked me home to my mother. Shaking, I couldn't speak for several minutes.

'After the war, we learned what happened to thousands of Hungarian Jews. The majority were taken to Auschwitz concentration camp, and we assume Asher went there too.

'I cannot bear to think of what my brother suffered, Julia, all because of the cruel and hateful Dorjan Halmi. All we know is that my dear Asher was one of over 440,000 innocent Hungarian Jews who didn't survive the war.

'Dorjan Halmi has to pay,' I added through clenched teeth.

Staring ahead, seeing yet again the look on Asher's face, I added, 'I cannot forgive him, Julia, and have thought that if I ever saw him alive, I would kill him, knowing it would cost me my own life. I wanted for numerous years to watch him die a slow and painful death like that inflicted on countless innocent members of my race. I know now, of course, that was a foolish idea, and something I would never have the courage to do. And anyway, it would not bring my Asher back. Even so, I never expected to see him again, not here in Australia and definitely not in little Wattle Creek.'

Getting agitated and starting to pace like a caged lion, I wanted to talk about anything but that man, so I explained to Julia about the yellow stars.

'There were restrictions placed on Jews, but none as humiliating as that which ensured that everyone recognised us. We were required to wear at all times a ten-centimetre yellow star, which had to be sewn onto the left side of all our jackets, overcoats, jumpers, etc.

'I'm sure you heard about those, even here in Australia.' Julia nodded. 'This made it easy for the people to report any Jews who were not following the regulations, and our fellow countrymen were encouraged to do so. Friends were turning against friends, neighbours against neighbours. Society as we had known it was disintegrating.

'The first day with the yellow stars, we were apprehensive about the reception from people on the street. The reaction wasn't easy to perceive, being almost non-existent. People looked at us curiously and kept their distance. We were relieved that there wasn't a hostile reaction, although we heard later that in some places Jews were attacked. However, on that day, we who mercifully were ignored noticed a distinct gulf between us who wore the Star of David and those who used to be our friends and fellow countrymen. They now regarded us as not worthy to breathe the same air.

'All jewellery, gold or silver and all pocket and wrist watches owned by Jews had to be delivered to the nearest bank, where receipts were given. Jew's property and businesses were also seized.

'Not all these regulations were adhered to by the Jews. Some had already hidden their valuables, while some handed their valuables to Gentile friends, who were to keep them until "it is over".

'Was your family able to keep everything safe, Louisa?'

'My father and mother had given jewellery and gold to friends for safekeeping, but the majority of these items were never returned to us because some of the people to whom they had been entrusted had disappeared. They had probably fled the war-torn country, as the economy had crashed, and the country was in ruins. Sadly, some denied to my mother and me that my father had given them anything. That hurt us the most as we had trusted these people, as previously they had been our friends.

But there is yet another reason why I had wished Dorjan dead, Julia.'

I paused.

'Several months later, he came for my mother and me,' I whispered, shuddering.

CHAPTER SEVEN

On the darkest day in November 1944, what we had feared happened. They came for my mother and me in the middle of the night, the usual time for arrests. Three members of the Arrow Cross party barged into our flat.

'We were arrested by Dorjan Halmi himself.'

I paused. My unseeing eyes fixed on the floor.

'A lot of people thought that all we needed to do to be safe was to register as members of a non-Israeli religion. My father believed it, and we became members of the Roman Catholic religion sometime towards the end of 1939.

'It is easy to say in hindsight that this was a coward's way to deal with the situation, but that is not true. For a Jew to become a Christian, in the hope that he and his family might be safe, was a greater sacrifice than to do nothing. No one but a Jew, Julia, can understand the anguish of the Jew who gives up his religion, which, while he may not practise it or believe it, was the faith of his ancestors.

'My mother experienced great distress when she had to get the signature of a Rabbi and his permission to abandon her faith and become a Catholic. He did not make it easy for her when he asked her how, after she betrayed her ancestors, she could ever visit her parents' graves.

'Unfortunately, the changing of religion did not prove to be effective in avoiding persecution, as we were defined as Jews by our race instead of by any religious affiliation. The distress my mother experienced was in vain.

'Even though we had been forced to wear the yellow stars, we still believed we had a measure of protection with our Catholic papers.

With shaking hands, my mother fumbled for these papers and showed them to the soldiers. Dorjan ripped them from my mother's hands and, while laughing, tore them to shreds in front of us.'

'I swore at him and promised him that one day I would find him and kill him. I can still see the sneer on his face and hear his mocking laugh. "You can't fool me. I know you are stinking Jews."

'We were then taken, shaking and crying, to the ghetto, a filthy, overcrowded place.'

Telling this story to Julia took about an hour. There were times of silence when I stared blankly, reliving the moments, and times when anger surged through me, driving me to circle the room again.

Julia went into my kitchen looking for some food. After inspecting my pantry and refrigerator, she grilled some cheese on toast and watched me as I ate it.

'This is delicious. Thank you,' I mumbled, mouth full. It had been quite a few days since I had eaten anything substantial. I had countless cups of tea and coffee, but had not thought about food, sure my stomach would not have welcomed it.

When talking with Julia, although she had not seen or experienced the things I shared, her empathy, love and understanding were like a soothing balm on a painful wound.

Over the years, I had tried to anaesthetise the pain by hurling myself into all-consuming projects, but it never had the effect I was seeking. Now, while sitting and talking, I could feel some lightness come into my soul, like a small candle flickering to life in a darkened room.

'Thanks, Julia, for caring enough to confront me, instead of allowing me to continue to wallow in my misery.'

I hoped that one day Julia might share her past with me, too.

We have been friends for more than thirty years, but neither of us has revealed anything about our younger days. We had wonderful memories of times when our children were young and we would all go on picnics and share camping adventures. Our children grew up together, and even today, they are close, like true cousins.

I had talked about how our country had suffered and how we Jews had been treated. With Julia's support, I wanted to explain myself to my book club friends. She wisely suggested that instead of trying to talk about my past and the reason for my reaction, it might be easier to write an explanation. I followed her advice and would give a copy to each member of the group. I expected a shocked response and possible coldness from some, one in particular, but I hoped for understanding.

Julia offered to help me prepare it over the next couple of days. When she left mid-afternoon, I flopped on the couch feeling drained and exhausted, and woke the following morning at milking time. With sand-filled eyes, I leaned my head against Bessie's warm flank as her milk slowly filled the bucket. I didn't mean to cry, but the drops kept falling, running down my face, unstoppable.

CHAPTER EIGHT

Julia arrived at about ten o'clock and found me busy doing nothing. She knew, in my sorry state, she needed to feed me still, so she kindly came with two fresh bread rolls.

Offering one to me, she quickly withdrew her outstretched hand. 'Oh, Louisa, I didn't think! These have ham in them!'

I reached out and, with a weak smile, took one.

'I'm not that Jewish, Julia. I have never been one to obey the rules. Thank you.' And I enjoyed every bite.

With cups of tea in our hands, we sat together on my swing chair, gazing at the mountains as I tried to prepare an explanation.

With pen and paper, Julia helped me start. 'Tell me about your childhood, Louisa. I'm surprised that in all the years I have known you, we have never talked about your years in Hungary. You would have had such a different upbringing from mine. I'm sorry I never asked.'

I told her I wouldn't have shared much if she had asked.

'I have managed to avoid talking about it for most of the years since I left Hungary. Not my favourite subject, for obvious reasons. I thought it was all behind me, until now.'

I decided to start at the beginning and tell her about my parents. I explained to her that my mother and father were, in hindsight, an unusual couple.

'Both my parents had busy lives. My father's work often took him away from Budapest, and our mother filled her days with her social club activities. This is one of the reasons why my brother and I were very close, as we only had each other. When not travelling, our father spent all his afternoons and evenings at the club and always had his dinner there. He perhaps thought, like most men of that era, that providing a home, food and education for his family was the beginning and end of his responsibilities.

'Our mother had little time for us, and we often felt like we were an inconvenience to her. She loved to be seen around town with the rich and famous and often had her picture in the local paper. She took no interest in our lives or our schooling, so we were a lot closer to the maids in the house than we were to our mother.

'We were considered rich when compared to the population around us. We had a car, a refrigerator and servants. My father had a successful business manufacturing farm machinery and had important government contracts in the agricultural industry.

'During the 1930s in the depression, my father's business flourished with the mechanisation of agriculture, while a great number of people were hungry and out of work. We were in the minority of Hungarians, living well. People who formerly had well-paid jobs were now begging for a piece of bread outside restaurants. People even collapsed on the streets from hunger.

'In the early years, my brother and I were insulated from the suffering, as we were very young.

'My parents did not talk much about being Jewish, although it had been mentioned, but it seemed to us to be of no consequence. They did not attend synagogue or any religious festivals. I think my mother was ashamed to mention her Jewish roots.

'The first realisation we had that being a Jew could be dangerous happened when I was fourteen and Asher was sixteen. My brother and I were walking one freezing winter's day by the lake near our house. We noticed some boys from Asher's school approaching. They started chanting, 'Büdös zsidó, Büdös zsidó, Büdös zsidó.'

'That means "Stinking Jew, stinking Jew, stinking Jew".
I found it hard to say the words and told Julia how we both had

tried to ignore them.

'That is shocking, Louisa. Kids can be so cruel, especially when they are in a group, egging each other on. How frightening for you both. What did you do? Did you run?'

I continued recounting that terrible day.

'I tried to hide my fear, looking at my shoes and the path ahead, as we quickened our pace. One of them jokingly suggested pushing Asher into the icy lake, and immediately, I heard the ice crack and a splash. The boys ran away as Asher struggled to climb out of the freezing water. The edges of the ice kept breaking off, and I was terrified that he would not be able to get out before he froze to death. It doesn't take long to die in such freezing water. I did what I could to help him, and then screamed to a couple of men nearby who ran over and pulled him out. They saved his life.

'We all knew this was life-threatening, and one of the men picked Asher up as we all ran towards our house. The other man ran faster ahead to warn our mother. Asher showed signs of hypothermia, gasping for air, shivering, dizzy and a little confused. My mother met us at the door with blankets and warm water. She removed Asher's ice-encrusted outer clothing and wrapped him in blankets, rubbing him vigorously all over and helping him to get some warm water inside his shaking body. A maid filled the bath with warm water, not hot, and soon he was lying in it, warming slowly. It took about twenty minutes for his violent shaking to subside and for his body temperature to rise, but he thankfully survived.

My parents knew the men who had helped us, and I heard that my father had compensated them handsomely, although they were reluctant to take any money.

We were both traumatised by the cruelty of Asher's foolish classmates, but I'm certain they didn't realise that he could have died. Since we didn't understand why he had been treated like this, we had no foreboding of what lay ahead for us Jews.

CHAPTER NINE

I had told Julia how my mother and I were taken to the ghetto, and she asked why we were not, like most Jews, sent to Auschwitz.

Then I shared the part of my story that still amazes me.

'One day in the ghetto, a man in the dreaded Arrow Cross uniform, locked his eyes on my mother, marched quickly towards us and roughly grabbed my mother's arm. Angry and hateful, he shouted at us in Hungarian. My mother's knees buckled, and I struggled to support her as we were forced, crying and shaking, into his van.

'The members of the Arrow Cross were terrifying, as their hatred of Jews was as visible to us as our yellow stars were to them. Thousands of Jews were murdered all over our city. To be shoved into a van by a man in that uniform meant certain death.

'Once inside the van, the man slammed the door, and then, after looking quickly around, turned to us with compassion in his eyes and whispered the most beautiful words we could never have imagined hearing.

'He spoke in Yiddish: 'ikh bin a iid du bist itst zikher'— 'I am a Jew. You are safe now.'

'He apologised for having frightened us, but he had to be careful. He disguised himself as a member of the Arrow Cross Party to rescue us, so he had to play the role of an arrogant and ruthless member of that party.

'We found out after the war that this brave man, Rabbi Pinchas Rosenbaum...'

I couldn't find my voice for some time, continually wiping

my eyes, trying to stem the flow of tears.

Taking a deep breath, I started. 'Pinchas Rosenbaum risked his life countless times to rescue his fellow Jews. He acquired an Arrow Cross uniform and, wearing this, not only enabled him to rescue Jews, but also to find out who would be taken next. He later acquired a German Gestapo uniform and, disguised as a German officer, obtained classified information, being fluent in both German and Hungarian. It is estimated that he saved thousands of lives, putting his own life in great peril every day. He was only 21, Julia, when the Germans invaded Hungary. Such selfless bravery.

'He took my mother and me to a place known as the "Glass House", a big building that used to be a glass factory. We were taken into a basement where other rescued families were staying. This is how this brave man, and others, saved thousands of us. The conditions were far from comfortable, being crowded with scarcely enough food. However, we were alive, and morale was high despite the conditions. Beyond the fact that we were saved, we realised that these people considered us worth saving. Looking back, I can still remember being overwhelmed by that feeling, having been treated for some time as less than human.'

'Your children must be fascinated by these stories, Louisa.'

I told Julia that my children did not know the details of my life in Hungary or how I came to be in Australia. They knew I was born there and came here in my late teens, but because I didn't talk about it, they didn't ask for details.

I told her, 'Over the years they had asked a few questions, but I had given them flippant answers that managed to stifle any curiosity. I had tried to convince myself that the past was the past, but if I had been honest with myself, I would have faced the fact that my past still haunted me.'

The time had come to write about my experiences, mostly for my children and grandchildren. They needed to know about their forefathers and the effects of the war on my homeland, and my people in particular. My children, of course, knew I was a

Jew, but since I never attended Jewish meetings, participated in the festivals or kept the food rules, they had not seen it relevant to their lives. I planned to give them a copy when they visited, and give an abridged version to my book club friends. Neither of my two children had shown any interest in any religion, which pleased me.

None of the ladies had any idea how or why the sound of that name had affected me. Julia had explained at the last book club meeting, which I had missed, that I knew the new owner of the supermarket in Hungary, and that hearing his name again had brought up some bad memories from the war. At my request, she had organised a meeting at her house, for me to apologise and explain my reaction. I worried that I might be forced to face that gentleman one day, but I didn't think I could ever have the strength to do that. I clung to the hope that he might soon leave town.

CHAPTER TEN

Julia's morning tea with the book club ladies was arranged for the following week. I planned to apologise for my behaviour and give them each a typed explanation, which Julia organised for Karen to copy at the church office. I hoped they would better understand what happened in Europe during the war, specifically to the Jews. My suffering was mild compared with that of thousands, but after sharing it with Julia, I developed a strong desire to tell my story, as the stories needed to be told, so the truth is never forgotten. It took hours to write and my vision was often blurred by tears. I relived painful experiences and once again felt the fear and panic rise in my heart, as my memories morphed into nightmares.

In the darkness, I stood on a cobbled street of Budapest, being taunted by a hate-filled Arrow Cross soldier, my feet immovable, stuck in treacle. Dorjan Halmi, with foul breath assaulting my face, shouted that he had killed my stinking Jewish brother and now would enjoy killing me. I screamed without sound, paralysed. He laughed at me, with lust-filled eyes, as he slowly drew his long, jagged dagger from its sheath.

This nightmare, which had stopped years ago, jolted me awake, my heart crashing against my ribs like a caged animal trying to escape. I sat in my kitchen hugging a mug of warm milk, reminding myself that it had been a dream and I now lived safely in Australia. Returning to bed, I tossed and turned until morning. Similar nightmares had the same effect on subsequent nights.

I had difficulty deciding what to include in my letter, throwing several crumpled pages into a bin. I wanted understanding, not sympathy, so some traumatic events had to be omitted. There were too many to write about and too many I wanted to forget.

My nerves jangled like a wind chime caught in a storm when I thought about the meeting. I knew some of the ladies were Christians, attending the church pastored by Karen's husband, so I wondered how they would respond. They were kind when I told them that I was Jewish, which gave me a measure of courage. I wasn't sure they would still accept me when they knew of the hatred I harboured for the man in the supermarket. When the day arrived, after a sleepless night, I had mixed feelings. I wanted these friends to know what happened in Hungary during the war, but I was reluctant to share Dorjan's part in it. I saw no way around it, as he was a major cause of my suffering then and now.

I wanted to give a bit of an introduction before handing out the printed story of my past. Looking at their faces, I found it hard to begin. With a pounding heart, my mind went blank. I felt like a small child about to present my first paper in front of the class. Julia had suggested that I write down an introduction, which I reluctantly did, with no intention of reading it. I smiled sheepishly at Julia as, with a shaking hand, I took the paper out of my pocket and unfolded it.

As I scanned the faces, I relaxed when I saw that Terror hadn't come. I moved my eyes to the back wall, composed myself, and then read my introduction.

CHAPTER ELEVEN

'Good morning to you all. I want to thank you for your patience with me and apologise to you for my rude behaviour. I know some of you phoned and some dropped by my house and I ignored you, and I am very sorry.

'I cannot excuse my behaviour, but I want to not just offer an apology but also try to explain why I acted the way I did. I have written some of my story and have a copy for each of you. For me, this has not been easy, but it has caused a measure of healing, and I hope it will give you some understanding, not just what I suffered, but what millions of innocent people endured in Europe during the Second World War.

'My story is about Hungary, but we Hungarians suffered for a far shorter time than the rest of Europe.

'As you know, I was born in Hungary and I spent my childhood and adolescence there. My name wasn't Louisa then, but Lilla Bálint. When I left Hungary, I planned to leave the past behind and start a new life. For that reason, I changed my name, foolishly thinking that such a superficial change could help to heal my heart.

'As I am 63 now, you know I lived in Hungary before and during the Second World War. Born in 1927, I turned 17 in 1944 when the Germans took over Hungary. I understand that most of the Western world was unaware of the events on the ground in Europe during that time, so I hope my story will explain some of the political details and parts of my personal experiences during that frightening time.

'I am taking this opportunity to tell you all these details, as

I have heard there have been moves, even now in 1990, to deny the horrors of the murders and torture of the Jews in Europe during the Second World War. We who are still alive and were eyewitnesses need to tell our story.

'In my years here in Australia, I assumed those events were behind me and would remain buried, but I have been thrust back into the horrors of those days by an event here in Wattle Creek.

'There is the mention of a certain person in my explanation, whom I had hoped never to hear about or see again. This Hungarian man is now the owner of our grocery shop on Main Street. I doubt I will ever go in there while he is there, and I hope you will understand when you read my story.

'Please remember that this is my story, and not yours. I suspect he has changed and no longer resembles the Dorjan from my past, so please don't treat him coldly or mention any of this to him. I mean it. He may be here in Australia, trying, like me, to leave his past behind. I hope you will agree when you read my explanation that facing him would be impossible for me, but it should not affect your relationship with him.

'I also want to emphasise that I expect you all to keep my letter confidential. This is not to be shared with anyone outside our group, except perhaps some parts with your family if you feel they can be trusted. I cannot emphasise this strongly enough. I want a solemn promise from each of you. It would be unfair to Dorjan to have his past broadcast throughout Wattle Creek. Some of us, I know, have secrets and regrets that, if they were gossiped around town, would devastate and humiliate us.'

Heads nodded.

'We must all allow him to leave his past behind and live a quiet life here like the rest of us. When his arrival was mentioned at our meeting, no one reacted negatively. Perhaps I am the only one who hasn't been to the supermarket to meet him. I am thankful to have heard from this group that he has moved here, instead of having the shock of unexpectedly seeing that man when buying my groceries. My experience of him is far removed from yours, and I am sure it will stay that way.

'When I heard his name at book club, the shock caused me to hide away like a turtle retreating into its shell. I couldn't cope with such unexpected news. Locking myself in my house did nothing to ease the pain, but it intensified. I am thankful to Julia for helping me to face it, and perhaps, in some way, find a way to deal with it.

'Please take this explanation home and read it at your leisure. I want you to also understand that the majority of Hungarians supported the Allies. We were all suffering because of the cruelty of the German government and wanted Hitler defeated. I have met older Australians who say they hate all Germans because of the atrocities of World War Two. They don't realise that, although the German leadership and the majority of the soldiers were brutal, Germans in general were and are good people. Most were unaware of the massacres and cruelty in the camps. You cannot judge the common people by their corrupt leader-ship. This applies to all nations and throughout world history.

'If you prefer not to take my explanation, that is fine. My aim is for you to have the opportunity to understand my behaviour and give you a glimpse into life in Europe during the Second World War. If we never mention it again, that is okay, but if any of you want to talk further, I can promise my door and telephone will be answered.'

I folded my piece of paper and put it back in my pocket as Karen handed out the copies to everyone there, and assured me that she would pass on copies to the people who couldn't make it for the morning tea.

We all sat chatting, eating sweet treats and drinking tea, as we do together at our regular book club meetings. Brenda had to leave and get back to the cafe, but as she was heading to the door, she called out to me, 'Well done, Louisa. I am going to sneak into my office and read this instead of dealing with the pile of paperwork that awaits me.' She laughed loudly as she waved goodbye to everyone.

I received warm hugs as others soon left, and assurances that they now understood my reaction and were keen to read what I had given them. Some said they were praying for me, but I didn't think that would do any good. The God of the Jews hadn't been there for us during the war, but it was sweet of them nonetheless.

Now I had to wait for possible reactions. The days that followed were difficult. I knew I had taken a risk, exposing my past and my feelings. I was convinced that it had been a bad mistake when, for several days, my phone remained silent and no one came to my door.

CHAPTER TWELVE

I caught a glimpse of Terror two or three times in the following week and knew she had a copy of my letter.

My dear friend and advocate, Julia, had already scheduled several days away with her family, and for me, her trip could not have come at a worse time.

We had no book club meeting that week due to a public holiday, for which I felt both pleased and disappointed. The silence was soothing and unsettling, like a quiet scene with hidden shadows, leaving me torn between peace and panic.

Six days later, I heard a faint knock on my door. I looked through the spy hole and saw Karen, the pastor's wife, the last person I would have expected to darken my door. I was sure she would have been repulsed by my bitter hatred of Dorjan and would have decided to keep her distance from such a sinner. Although she was kind during our book club meetings, I expected her to treat me differently now. I heaved a sigh and thought, 'Here we go, the Bible basher. I'm in for a lecture.'

I reluctantly invited her in.

I was sure that she would say I had to stop being hateful and unforgiving and that I must go to her church and get my life straightened out. She would tell me how wicked I was and that I was headed for hell, and deserved to be sent there. With my guns loaded, I stiffened, ready to let my own bullets fly.

But she said none of those things. Instead, she asked me how I felt and said she admired my courage in sharing my past. She caught me off guard, disarming me.

'Louisa, I was moved by your letter and from reading it, I

feel I know you more and have a clearer understanding of the horrific life you endured in Europe during the war. I'm sorry to hear that you suffered so much. You were not much more than a child.'

She asked me about my first impressions of Australia, and we laughed together about some silly things that I can't even remember. I made a pot of tea to have with the chocolate biscuits she brought, and after chatting together for about half an hour, we walked together in my garden discussing the different flowers and vegetables and the best breed of hens for laying. I was surprised at how normal she was.

Her kindness intrigued me as she wasn't acting like the preachers' wives I had met in Hungary. Those women were not the sort of people I would invite to my home—a supercilious group, rigid and unfeeling, as if forged from stone and coated in a thick layer of ice.

When some Christians in Hungary heard I was a Jew, they considered me no longer worthy of their time. One said my people killed Jesus, and so we were all cursed. My generation had nothing to do with the killing of some prophet hundreds of years ago. They seemed to be an irrational bunch, and I had long been determined to avoid them whenever possible.

I was told that Jews were no longer special to God since they murdered Jesus. Therefore, the church had replaced Israel as God's special people. I didn't know about any of that, so I ignored it. I hadn't seen any signs of being special to God, as I had witnessed the opposite in the war. The less I saw of Christians and nasty pastor's wives, the better.

But I heard myself asking Karen to please come again soon—and I meant it— as I waved 'goodbye'. She left laden down with flowers, vegetables and three litres of milk for her boys.

Since the visit from Karen, I wondered if perhaps some pastor's wives might be okay. One anyway.

Another visitor that day was most welcome.

Late in the afternoon, with arms open wide and a warm

smile, Brenda rushed up my steps, wrapped me in her arms and lifted me off the verandah.

At our first book club meeting, we heard a loud and animated summary from Brenda. She runs the popular local café, Common Ground, and she is perfect for the place.

Entering the cafe, our senses are always bombarded with the aroma of freshly brewed coffee and the smell of warm pastries. It has the atmosphere of a cosy lounge room with comfortable couches and chairs of varying styles and colours, some well-worn and some new. A gifted bargain hunter, Brenda found most of her decorations and furniture at garage sales and second-hand shops and a few pieces on the side of the road, waiting for the council's monthly collection.

I have enjoyed countless cups of coffee there. Fortunately, she can leave the cafe in the hands of her assistant and join us for the book club meetings once a week. She didn't give any details about herself then, and none of us felt free at our first meeting to ask questions. Despite her vibrant personality, I could sense a profound depth in her. She reminded me of a rushing river full of energy, but deep below the surface, where the water creeps silently, deep thoughts and perhaps secrets are hiding beneath her lively, outgoing personality. I was delighted by her visit.

'I've dropped by for a cuppa at your place for a change,' she said, then threw her head back with a hearty laugh.

Over cups of my inferior coffee and a slice of her lemon cake, Brenda shared funny stories about some of her regular customers. She never mentioned any of these people by name, as she is fond of them all.

One trait I love about Brenda is that she can have me laughing one moment and then transition seamlessly into a deep discussion.

With a pause in our conversation, Brenda mentioned how reading about the horrors I had lived through made her sad. She leant back on my couch, put her feet up on my coffee table and settled in for a good chat.

'Louisa,' she said, 'could you tell me more about your life during the war? I want to know what it was like to be a Jew in Hungary in those years. I enjoy history, and it's great to be able to hear it from someone who experienced it. I would also love to hear how it affected your family in particular. Australia is so isolated from the rest of the world that I am sure my parents' generation had no idea what was happening in Hungary during the war. If you feel comfortable, that is, as I know it brings up painful memories.'

'It's doing me good to talk about it, Brenda, so, since you like history, I'll start with a bit of a history lesson.

CHAPTER THIRTEEN

'Brenda, this is hard to believe, but back in 1920, in Versailles, two medium-ranking Hungarian officials signed away two-thirds of our country and 3.3 million of our citizens. I don't know how they had the power to do that; in fact, I don't think they did. But they did it anyway, and it seemed no one had the power to reverse it.

'It was called the Treaty of Trianon and was one of the cruellest, most absurd treaties ever signed, and the greatest tragedy in Hungary's 1000-year history. France and England wanted to annihilate the strong Austro-Hungarian monarchy, so we lost not just land but almost all our natural resources, as well as our industries, our defence force and our navy. The treaty destroyed our country in every way possible.'

'That is shocking, Louisa. I hate hearing about government greed, where leaders willingly destroy their homeland for their own ends, with no regard for the common people or the effect on future generations. Please continue, Louisa. I know the worst is yet to come.'

'In 1933, cunning Hitler gained Hungary's loyalty by arranging the return of some of these territories. This smart move resulted in our leaders being willing to support Hitler and marked the beginning of increased anti-Jewish legislation.

'Despite the changes being slow and seemingly insignificant at first, it became obvious to anybody but the blind and the young, like my brother and I, that being a Jew would deny us a normal life, although no one could dream of the holocaust to follow.

'In the first years of war in Europe, my brother and I were still in school. My parents chose to give up their Jewish heritage and become Roman Catholic, in the hope of sidestepping the persecution. I attended a Catholic school but had no interest in that religion, or any religion for that matter. It was a place where hypocrisy and cruelty thrived. The nuns were cruel to everyone, but mostly to us Jews. Once they found out we were Jewish, they intensified their punishments, and we were often beaten for no reason. I hated every minute I was there. My parents had heard it was a school with a prestigious reputation, and that was all they cared about. I think they chose not to believe half of the things I told them, as the nuns would smile sweetly and act humble and kind whenever they talked to them. Wicked, nasty people.'

I didn't want to talk about them any more as it made me angry, so I went to the kitchen, made two more cups of coffee, and then continued with the history.

'The terrible treatment of the Hungarian Jews was concentrated at first on areas outside of Budapest, where the first ghettos were set up. As a teenager, I wasn't affected, but the stories my parents heard were disturbing.

'As the war progressed, the Hungarian authorities became stronger supporters of Germany. In December 1941, Hungary joined the Axis Powers in declaring war against the United States, and cut us off from any relationship with the West.

'There were battles in which Germany suffered defeat and in which Hungary lost tens of thousands of soldiers. The Germans put our men on the front lines, so the Hungarian army was virtually wiped out.

'At this time, the Regent of Hungary, Miklos Horthy, began trying to back out of the alliance with Germany. This displeased Hitler, so in March 1944, German troops invaded Hungary to keep the country loyal by force.

'Hitler then set up a new government, faithful to Germany, with Hungary's wicked former ambassador to Germany, Ferenc Szalasi, the leader of the Arrow Cross party, as the Prime Minister. He was a wicked, heartless man.

'Germany took over the country without a bullet being fired. Some days before, an unusual number of German students came for their 'holiday' to Hungary and German soldiers 'happened' to be travelling through Hungary to Russia and Yugoslavia. It was clearly a well-planned 'peaceful' invasion.

'Suddenly, our government was under the complete control of Hitler. I remember watching the streets fill with German soldiers, which I thought was strange. I noticed people were scared as they rushed home.

'That night my father was home, which was unusual, and he was in a rage. He said our country had been invaded and taken over by Hitler. He warned that there would be bad days ahead, as he didn't trust Hitler. My father was close to Hungary's top government officials, and some of his friends were suddenly missing. Seeing my father like that was frightening. He was a man who always had control over every area of his life. His inability to do anything to stop what was happening to our country was driving him mad. I had never seen my father so frustrated and helpless. He paced the floor for hours, sometimes shouting and sometimes muttering under his breath. My mother, Asher and I could only watch in silence, not daring to speak. My father had a more realistic premonition of what lay ahead than most, because of the government and business circles he moved in.

'Szalasi was such an evil man, who co-operated with the Germans and employed his Arrow Cross thugs to murder Jews, often throwing their bodies in the Danube River. Even decades after the war, some remains of these victims have been found. He was held responsible for the murder of at least thirty-five thousand innocent Jews, and tens of thousands being sent to the ghettos and on the death marches. He turned his 163 days in power into a nightmare for my country.

'After the war, U.S. troops captured Szalasi in Germany and returned him to Hungary, where the People's Tribunal sentenced him to death in 1946 and hanged him in public for treason. I don't think any Hungarian people felt sorry for him.'

Through gritted teeth I told Brenda that I would hate him until my dying day, and how pleased I had been when I heard he had been hanged, although I would have preferred a more painful slow death, like he inflicted on others, including my own family and friends.

I grinned. 'My father knew Szalasi and hated him. I'm sure he would have enjoyed watching his public execution.'

I thought she would agree with me and join me in my justified hatred of the man, but she just smiled and patted my hand.

I took a break from all the history and asked Brenda how the cafe was going.

'It's going well, Louisa. I'm surprised how popular it is. I am happy that I can provide some work for a few home bakers in town who keep me well supplied with fresh cakes and scones. I enjoy hearing all the local news from my regular customers, and especially enjoy chatting with those who drop in every morning for their tea or coffee. I like to think that I give them a cheerful start to their day.

'Roger does a great job in the kitchen and has been with me for years. I couldn't run it without him. I learnt how to run a coffee shop years ago when I lived in Sydney, and back then decided there was nothing I would rather do than run my own. A country town is the perfect place as the customers are regular and most of them are like neighbours. I feel blessed to be able to work at a job I love.

'Now, back to you. Your story is more interesting than mine. Would you mind telling me what it was like to be a Jew in Hungary, or are you tired of recalling all these things? I must admit, I think you are the first Jew I have ever met!'

Brenda laughed loudly again. Blunt but always kind.

'I don't know many people who would be interested in all this history, Brenda.'

So, I finished my coffee and began again.

'Up until Szalasi's appointment, Budapest had been a relatively safe place for us Jews, but less than a week after the German occupation, in March 1944, new restrictions were posted in the papers and stuck on the walls of buildings. Jews could not leave their homes between 7 pm and 7 am, must not travel in cars, must travel in the rear of trams, must not go further than five kilometres from home and must shop only between 3 and 4 pm. Harsh restrictions that we didn't understand. I don't know what they thought would happen if we shopped at different hours, or rode in cars!

'All cameras, telephones and radios owned by Jews had to be delivered to the nearest police station. In this way, we were prevented from having any contact with the outside world, and people outside of Europe remained ignorant of the atrocities in Hungary.

'In my letter, I told you about the yellow stars. There were a lot of other restrictions too. By mid-April, Jewish children were no longer allowed to attend school.'

Brenda planted her feet on the floor and sat forward as though she couldn't believe what I had said. 'What? They had to quit school?'

'Yes, I had left school the previous year and had my diploma, but young friends and relatives thought it was great news, and they expected to have an enjoyable holiday. They had no idea….'

'What happened to your dad, Louisa? You told me how upset he was when the German soldiers came into Hungary, but you haven't mentioned that he came to Australia with you.'

Eyes on the floor, I said, 'No, Brenda. He didn't come with us. Can I tell you all about that another time?'

'Oh yes, of course. I'm sorry, Louisa. I am being insensitive. Thank you for sharing all this with me. I feel privileged to know what you have lived through.

'Now I think it is time for me to go and visit Bessie and see what I can steal from your veggie garden.'

I always enjoyed her laugh, and felt Brenda and I, although very different, were becoming close friends.

The day after Brenda's visit, I heard something from my tennis partner, Irene, that hit me like a serve I wasn't ready for.

CHAPTER FOURTEEN

I have known Irene for quite some time at tennis and was pleased to hear she would be part of the book club. Despite playing tennis together, our conversations had been superficial.

Irene is fit at fifty-seven, as she plays various sports and is a member of our town's gym. Married to the mayor, she has never lived anywhere except Wattle Creek. They have four adult children who have moved to the city for work. She is competitive and often anxious, but still good company. Irene had been at the special meeting at Julia's, but I hadn't seen her since.

On Thursday, I arrived ready to play, catching a brief flicker of surprise on Irene's face. She may have expected me to have locked myself away again. It was tempting, but the effects of the last time were not easy to forget.

We played two sets of enjoyable tennis and went to the clubhouse for a cool drink. Over glasses of creamy iced coffee, she talked about my letter, saying she felt sorry that she had no idea what my life had been like in Hungary.

'Irene, I assure you it was my fault since I had kept my past securely locked away and would have given you a flippant answer if you had asked.'

We talked together for a while with some of the other players, and when they left, we had a second drink together.

She then lowered her eyes, while her hands fidgeted with her serviette. I sensed she had rehearsed what she was about to say.

She took a shaky breath and began, 'I want to tell you something that I have not told anyone. Since you were brave enough to share your pain, I have now found the courage to share my secret with you.'

For a full minute, she remained silent, looking at her hands, before taking a deep breath.

Tears pooled in her eyes as she stammered, 'My husband often yells at me for hours, Louisa, and I am scared that he may hit me. I don't know what has triggered this behaviour, and I don't know what I am doing wrong.'

She appeared to be tired in both body and soul. The air left her lungs with a deep sigh, her shoulders sagging with the release of a burden she had carried alone for far too long.

I didn't know what to say or how to comfort her, but I assured her it wasn't her fault and she should not blame herself.

I understood to some extent the pain she suffered and the courage needed to put deep pain into words.

'My sports and gym activities are an excuse to leave the house every day.'

Staring at the floor still, she added, 'He has been retired for five years now, and they have been the worst of my life. I love him, but I cannot bear to continue to live like this.'

She looked at me with pleading eyes as she waited for my advice. Her husband, as the mayor of our town, is a respected member of our community. I had never heard a negative word about him and felt certain no one suspected he was a raging bear at home.

I had read about people like this before, who seem to have two different personalities, one in private and one in public. Some women have husbands like this and are afraid to tell anyone, as their husbands are usually popular, often the life of the party and the perfect gentleman in public, but a monster to his family at home. These poor wives know that no one will believe them.

With a surge of inspiration, I said, 'How about talking to Karen?'

I didn't know a lot about churchy people, but Karen was always kind and seemed to have some wisdom. Irene brightened at that suggestion and admitted she could see something different in her. I was curious to hear what Karen said, hoping she would not tell Irene to continue to live with this abusive man as it was 'her cross to bear'. I had heard that weird expression from a Christian soon after coming to Australia. It sounded so stupid that I was surprised I remembered it.

I hugged her before we left the clubhouse. She seemed to be experiencing the same release I had felt when I shared my story with Julia.

Feeling pleased as I headed home, I looked forward to a cool shower and a relaxing afternoon reading the week's book for book club. I hoped that more good things might come from my confession, as perhaps others, like Irene, would feel free to share personal struggles. I still managed to avoid the supermarket, as I now had my groceries delivered, which had become a welcome convenience. Life had returned to a predictable rhythm, or so I thought.

As I drove along my familiar street towards home, thinking about our current 'who-done-it?' mystery called, *You Think You Know*, horror and panic gripped me as my house came into view, almost causing me to swerve into a tree. On my letterbox, I saw a large, hideous yellow star.

CHAPTER FIFTEEN

Outraged, I grabbed the star and shredded it, and without knocking, barged into Julia's house, calling her name. She came running towards me, eyes wide as I threw the torn star at her feet, waves of panic washing over me, leaving me breathless.

'On my letterbox,' was all I said.

Julia dropped to her knees, scooping up the pieces. 'Oh no. Oh no. Who would do such a thing?'

I had no doubt.

'Of course we know, Julia.'

'We can't be certain that Terry is responsible, Louisa.'

'I saw that look on her face, Julia. I heard her condescending comment at our first book club meeting. I know.'

I needed to plan my revenge, determined that Terror wasn't getting away with this.

My schemes escalated as I paced, from writing a hateful note, poisoning her beautiful rose bushes, killing her beloved dog, to burning her house down. In my irrational state, these all seemed great ideas, and no less than she deserved.

Julia calmly listened to my hare-brained ideas, hoping I would soon calm down. In our long friendship, I knew she had never seen me behave like this.

When I finally slumped on her couch, tears escaping, she brought me a hot drink and sat with me. I could feel my pulse thudding, fuelled by rage.

'Julia, what am I to do?' I pleaded.

'I can't ignore it. I can't let her get away with it. At least half the town will have seen it. Can I walk the streets without people staring at me, even spitting at me? Maybe I should leave town, now that the whole town has heard I am a Jew and everyone now hates me.'

'Louisa. Stop. Stop,' Julia was almost shouting.

'You are not in Hungary now, and there are no Jew-hating Arrow Cross soldiers walking our streets. That world is far behind you. Please try and relax.'

With the teacup drained, I shared my plan.

'First, a threatening letter, then I'll see if she settles down.'

Without Julia's support, I still thought it was brilliant.

'If I get no apology and things like this continue, I will move to plan B. Perhaps a rose bush or two will be sacrificed. That will teach her that I mean business.'

Julia looked worried, but let me ramble on, devising numerous self-justified schemes for revenge.

I thanked Julia for listening and walked home an hour later. Before I left, Julia mentioned that she would pray for me, which surprised me. In all of the years we had lived near each other, she had never mentioned prayer, and as far as I knew, she had never been to a church. I suggested she pray for Terror as she would need it after I had finished with her. Although upset, I found comfort in my plans.

I wrote my letter before I slept and placed it in Terry's letterbox as the first pink rays of dawn were painting the clouds.

Then I waited for a response.

I spent the day doing my usual chores, enjoying my garden and animals, surprised at the peace I felt. Towards evening, I dropped in to see Julia to apologise for my rant the day before.

She listened patiently as I found myself, after apologising without a hint of sincerity, continuing to share my plans for revenge, but with less emotion. After a light dinner with Julia, I headed home.

I found another hate-filled star attached to my letterbox. I tore it up as I glared towards Terry's house and saw a slight movement of the curtain at her front window. She had been watching, and I knew she was gloating. I slept fitfully that night as I rehearsed more plans. Plan A had not been strong enough. I would watch for the right moment to execute another plan.

CHAPTER SIXTEEN

The following day, we had our book club meeting, but Terror didn't come. I casually asked if anyone had heard from her, and Karen said Terry had a doctor's appointment. Sneaky, I thought.

We had an enjoyable meeting discussing the book we had been reading, a thrilling mystery called *The Wrong Tree*. The end of the book had an unexpected twist, shocking the readers into realising they had been suspecting an innocent person.

Some of the ladies made a point of chatting with me about my experiences in Hungary. They offered sympathy, and appreciation for what I had shared. Some had questions and wanted to hear more of my story and my perspective on the war.

No one mentioned the stars on my letterbox, so I presumed no one had seen them, which was a relief.

One lady in the group interested me at our first meeting, and I was keen to get to know her. I felt she may be a kindred spirit, perhaps also dealing with hidden pain.

When Rosa introduced herself, she told us she had taught computer science over the years in various universities and had taken early retirement, but I heard she has been asked to speak at conferences around the world. I knew nothing about computers and didn't own one, although my son and daughter had recently purchased one each for their homes, but I wasn't sure what they would use them for.

I decided to invite Rosa to join me for lunch to help get my mind off Terror and the stars. She arrived with some cherries from her tree, which we munched after having my cauliflower soup and buttered toast.

I asked Rosa about her life, but she talked about her education and her work experience and nothing about her family. She tried to teach me about the benefits of computers, but it was way over my head. I didn't feel I would have any use for one, even if I could figure out how to use it.

I had heard her called 'Mrs Campbell' but didn't know if she was divorced or widowed.

Before Rosa left, we took a walk in my garden, which covers most of my backyard, with the two fenced paddocks behind it. Bessie occupies one paddock, and my pet chickens cluck contentedly in the one beside Bessie's, producing sufficient eggs for me to share with friends.

Rosa admired my piece of heaven, and I sent her home with some milk, spinach and eggs.

She left for another conference later in the week and ten days later invited me for lunch. Her two-story house was nestled amongst towering shady trees and well-manicured gardens with a small orchard behind the house. It was at the opposite end of town from my place, so I had not seen it before. It was magnificent.

Rosa seemed relaxed as the hostess, and while eating lunch, I commented on a picture of a man in his late twenties above the impressive stone fireplace.

'That is not my son,' she said. 'Steve was my husband.' She added after a pause, 'He died in a light plane crash, while crop-dusting a field where the power lines were unmarked. We had been married for less than two years.'

The ache in her heart poured out her eyes, and I reached for her hand.

She whispered, 'Our baby was stillborn three weeks after he died.'

Tears filled my eyes as I hugged her. Oh, poor Rosa with no outward scars but invisible pain, which seemed to be more common than I had realised.

We both knew pain, so I wanted to be the best friend I could be to Rosa, a fellow sufferer.

She had been away when I handed out my explanation at the meeting at Julia's, but her sister, Charlotte, had taken a copy for her. She said she understood when she heard I had hidden away for two miserable weeks.

'I did the same, Louisa, hiding away for many desolate weeks after the death of my husband and baby. I had also assumed it was the best way to cope with the shock and pain.

'Like you, I did not find it helpful,' she added with a hint of a smile. 'Solitude did not have the desired effect that either of us had anticipated, right, Louisa? Talking with people who loved me and accepting their condolences and kindness did more to help me through the nightmare than locking myself away.'

She talked for quite a while about her husband. He had been a pilot in the Air Force after he left school, and left the Air Force to be a private pilot just before they were married.

'He hoped to fly private planes for the rich and famous and had turned down a job with someone in Sydney, as he preferred country living and thought Wattle Creek would be the ideal place to raise our family. So, he had just turned to crop dusting as a way to continue flying, which he loved.'

She told me that she rarely talks about Steve, as many people do not understand the pain of losing someone so dear.

'I know you understand, Louisa, and I think you and I will be good for each other.' She smiled and hugged me as we walked to my car. I left her house late in the afternoon and invited Rosa to drop in on Monday if she had time.

After I reached home, my weekly grocery order arrived. I found a few items I had not ordered—expensive things that I bought as occasional treats. Two jars of posh coffee that are beyond my budget, some Belgian chocolate and two pieces of rib-eye steak, so I called the supermarket to ask for someone to come and collect them.

The lady checked her notes and confirmed that these items were ordered and were definitely to be delivered to me. I assured her that there had been a mistake, but she said they had been paid for, but she could not tell me the purchaser's name. I was touched by a friend's anonymous gift.

Julia came for dinner and we barbecued the two rib-eye steaks and then relaxed, nibbling on the chocolate. When I told Julia about the mystery food, I watched her reaction closely, but she was as surprised as I was by this gift. Neither of us could guess who paid for these items, and I admit I enjoyed the treats more, not knowing to whom I was indebted.

The following week passed with no incidents to upset me. There were no more stars or surprises in my groceries, so my life returned to its pleasant rhythm. The weather was warm and pleasant, and I was spending longer on my walks and more time in the garden. I hadn't noticed Terry peering at me from behind her curtains, and I had received no complaints from her for a while. I was starting to hope that her sickness had mellowed her, but deep down, I doubted it. I was just thankful for the break. The following week I had two visitors and again relived some painful experiences from my past.

CHAPTER SEVENTEEN

Rosa dropped by for a chat on Monday. I asked her about her husband, Steve, and how they had met and what he was like. With these couple of questions, I felt that I had somehow released the memories that she had locked away in her heart. She spoke for some time about their first meeting in a bar when they were both in the Air Force. I was surprised to hear that she had enlisted too. She said she went to university while in the Air Force, and that was how she was able to study science, followed by a degree in computer studies, back when computer science was in its infancy. She told me that some things recently available on computers have been used by the military for quite some years. She said that she and Steve hit it off straight away and were married within a year. Her time with him had been the happiest years of her life. She described him as a fun-loving man and a bit of a daredevil.

'I don't think there was anything he was afraid of. Even his friends told me he was an amazing pilot and he would always be the first one to try a new manoeuvre.'

Her eyes shone with love and pride as she talked.

'He was a wonderful husband and always so kind to me. He was overjoyed about becoming a dad, and I know he would have been a wonderful one.

'He wasn't always so well-behaved, Louisa. He was a drug addict and dealer for a few years, and it was the desire to kick that habit that caused him to join the military. He told me he needed accountability to keep him away from the drugs. He felt he didn't have the willpower to resist them, but knew the consequences would be terrible if they were found in his possession when in the Air Force. He stopped using and selling them a few months before he enlisted, and never touched them again.'

She then asked me about my husband, knowing that I also was a widow. We were from different generations, but we shared a lot of the same pain. We had both lost our beloved husbands suddenly in an accident. I was thankful for the years I had with Andrew, having heard that Rosa had less than two years with her Steve.

'Rosa, one of the hardest things I had to deal with was the torture of the 'if onlys'.

She stood up and paced the room.

'Oh, Louisa, few people know how that feels. You are the first person I have spoken to who under-stands first-hand what I went through.'

I told her about the blocked guttering and my suggestion to call someone to clear it for us, and she groaned with understanding.

She said, 'All we could do was try our best to stop our minds from going there, but it was such a battle especially soon after Steve's accident! I wanted someone to pay for the negligence, but I knew it wouldn't bring Steve back.'

As we finished our tea, there came a loud knock and 'Hello. Anyone home?' It must surely be pink-haired Brenda, and Rosa and I were both pleased to see her, ready for a distraction.

Brenda went straight to the kitchen and then relaxed with a cup of tea and jumped straight in.

'So, Louisa, I'm guessing Rosa wants to hear more about your time in Hungary, too. How about you tell us both the story about your dad? What do you think? Is now okay for you?'

Rosa looked shocked and then smiled. We were both getting used to Brenda's direct approach.

'Okay,' I said, smiling, 'But you will have to first make Rosa and me another cup of tea.

She grabbed our mugs and went to the kitchen, making

plenty of noise, searching for biscuits or cake.

When she came back with our tea and a packet of Tim Tams, I started my story.

In my letter, I described what happened when I was a child in Hungary. Also, I explained my family's social position. When Germany took over Hungary, things went downhill fast.

'Soon after the Germans came, they arrested our father on a false charge. We were devastated as he had friends in high places in the government, so we thought he would be safe. He helped with the supply of weapons to the army as he owned machinery shops that were converted for the purpose. His only crime was that he was Jewish.

'One day, we waited for him to return from work, as usual, and as night fell, we became concerned. We wanted to believe he was working late. However, we waited all night, and before morning, we knew that something terrible had happened to him. My brother bravely walked to his factory, but as he approached, he saw crowds of soldiers. The Germans had taken over the factory, and he did not dare to venture any closer.

'My mother became hysterical and spent a week in bed.

'From our careful enquiries, we found out he had been arrested and charged with something ridiculous, but we could not find out where he had been taken, and even after the war, we were unable to get any information.

'Not long after my father's disappearance, my brother was forced to join the Fire Brigade as he had not joined the Hungarian Youth Army, which was similar to Hitler Youth.

'My mother and I were alone and felt defenceless as we rarely saw Asher. The torture of not knowing what happened to my father or what might happen in our country weighed heavily on us night and day. We hardly thought or talked about anything else.'

Rosa asked, 'Can you tell us a bit about your mother, Louisa? She had lost her husband and worried about her son. All this trauma in her life must have affected her. Did it change her in any way?'

'Oh yes! As I have mentioned, we were quite affluent, and this caused my mother to be, as you say in English, a snob.' I smiled.

'After the disappearance of my father, Mum and I became close, grieving together. We did not know whether my father was alive, dead or being tortured. My harsh mother softened during our suffering. For the first time, her eyes were opened to the hardship around her, and she became aware of her ingratitude for what and who she had in her life.

'All my life, my mother had been focused on her social position, her wealth and her possessions. Asher and I knew these things were more important to her than her children. When her status and her wealth vanished, her sole concern was to get food and stay warm.

'It is not easy to describe the anguish we lived with night and day. After my brother disappeared, which you read about in my letter, Mum and I stayed off the streets as much as possible. We were then living in a flat owned by my parents instead of our house, as we thought we were well-hidden. Of course, no one knew how or when this nightmare would end, so we all lived in a constant state of anxiety.

'Having converted to Roman Catholicism did not ensure safety. We were now wearing the shameful yellow star, enforced after the German occupation. Since we looked like Jews and our friends and acquaintances knew we were Jews, we could not avoid it. It is interesting that at a time like that, you discover who your true friends are. My parents had acquaintances and business contacts but no true friends. These all vanished when being Jewish was vilified, and my mother felt betrayed by people who she and Dad thought were their friends. I don't think that up until that time, my mother knew what a true friend was.

'I know my transformed mother would have loved you two. Before the war, she might have looked down on you as inferior. After the war, and when we arrived in Australia, she had changed. She had come to love and appreciate all people, so something worthwhile came out of our terrifying experiences. My mother experienced true friendship when we came to Australia as refugees. All classes were thrown together in the refugee camp, and my mother was very popular. She could speak several languages, so she reached out to the confused and frightened people. It is strange to say, but she came alive there. It wasn't an easy time, but for the first time in her life, my mother became useful, as she was able to help those who were struggling to communicate. In a way, she felt fulfilled in that place as she was able to make a valuable contribution to the people around her.

'The war did not have this effect on all survivors. Some have said they have no faith in the human race, and now see all people as animals.'

I had talked enough, and we all walked outside into the vegetable garden. I sent them both home with milk, eggs and flowers.

It surprised me over the following week to see Karen visit Terry on at least three occasions, so I hoped she was straightening her out.

Terror seemed to be staying home more than usual, and I noticed once again she was peering through her curtains whenever I left or arrived home. It was getting creepy.

CHAPTER EIGHTEEN

We read a light-hearted book called *Bickering Bakers*, based on a book club in Britain where the ladies competed against each other to bake the fanciest treats. The snacks soon became the focus of their meetings, with some hilarious cooking disasters along with some touching life lessons.

There was one member of their group who had never baked anything, and another who had been a teacher in a pastry chef's school and had won prizes for her baked goods. The expert was insensitive to the non-baker and turned her nose up at her first attempts. She would critique her biscuits and brownies and refuse to taste them. This resulted in the novice baker leaving the group. It was a harsh lesson for the chef when she realised what she had done. The other members of the group pointed out how unfeeling and cruel she had been. They all realised how competing against each other had been destructive to their relationships and the book club. They had lost their focus for meeting together. It was supposed to be a fun group, sharing books and their lives, but it had become so competitive that some confessed that they did not enjoy coming anymore. The professional chef humbled herself and visited the non-baker and asked her for forgiveness. She then offered to teach her how to bake, and they became firm friends, even with the expert also having some failures. By the end of the book, the book club ladies could not tell what was baked by the expert and what was made by her student, and they no longer competed against each other but appreciated everyone's contributions.

Most of us found baking therapeutic, and we had never considered competing against each other, as we all shared our recipes. *Bickering Bakers* contained several recipes, from easy to expert, and we decided to try some.

Brenda said, 'Hey, how about the more stressed we feel, the more difficult the recipe we try? And we must bring it along for all to taste.'

Everyone loved the idea, perhaps thinking they would not need to try a hard one anytime soon.

Three weeks had passed since the stars and the mystery groceries had arrived, so I started to settle down, believing the foolish prank was now behind me.

Terry came to a couple of the meetings and smiled at me sheepishly, but did not comment on my hostile epistle. She didn't look well, but I was not convinced she was very sick.

However, the day after the *Bickering Bakers* meeting, another ugly star appeared. Terry may have been unwell, but her clever scheme to hide her true agenda could not fool me. A tidal wave of fury swept over me — time again for action.

I strutted over to Terry's house and pounded on her door until she eventually opened it.

'Okay, Terry. Enough is enough. I know you hate me, and you hate Jews, but if this doesn't stop, I am calling the police. I got your message with the first yellow star.'

Shaking and shifting my weight from one foot to the other, giving her no chance to respond, I spun around and stamped down her steps. I prided myself on my calm and easy-going nature, so these recurring eruptions of fury stunned me. Yet I managed to convince myself that my reactions were justified. I preferred to avoid confrontation, but Terry's actions were disturbing me at such a profound level that I hoped my threat would have the desired effect. I wasn't intending to go to the police, as I didn't want any more people to know about the stars. I planned to keep this nonsense as quiet as possible, hoping this would be the end of it.

Terror missed our meeting the following week, and we were told she was quite ill. The news did not soften my heart. Maybe she wasn't pretending to be sick, but not too sick to put stars on my letterbox, two of which appeared in the following week. Maybe Karen was often dropping by to see Terry because she was sicker than I was prepared to accept.

I was getting so frustrated that I made a difficult recipe from *Bickering Bakers* for our next meeting.

It was called "Baklava" and I had never heard of it before. It is a sweet and sticky treat made of layers of flaky filo pastry filled with crushed nuts, and sweetened with honey.

Mine didn't look as fancy as the picture in the book, but it tasted pretty good.

Brenda was so impressed that she asked me if I would make it for the cafe.

'No way, Brenda. I'll never make that again. It was far too much work.'

Two days later, my self-righteous attitude crumbled like a sandcastle hit by an unexpected wave. I would never be the same after what I saw.

CHAPTER NINETEEN

I was working in my garden near my side fence one sunny afternoon planting strawberry seedlings, Gypsy was sticking her nose in my way as I chatted to her, telling her about the delicious crop my seedlings would produce. A kookaburra was laughing in a tree nearby, singing along with the crowing of my rooster. Life was good. I saw a movement near my fence and glanced up to see a boy rush towards my letterbox, attach a star, remount his bicycle and speed away. I was shocked to see Terry had hired someone to do her dirty work. Gritting my teeth, I stood and dropped my little spade, about to storm over to Terry's house again.

Moments later, I saw Terry leave her house, hobble towards my letterbox and remove the star. She tore it in two and shuffled home, in pain with every slow step.

I fell to my knees and then lay sprawled on the grass, taking shallow breaths, with my heart pounding with the frantic rhythm of a runaway horse's hooves on a cobbled street. I replayed the scenes from the previous weeks with the sickening revelation that when Terry was watching through her window, she wanted to protect me from further hurt. The stars appeared when she was too sick to destroy them. Terry's behaviour puzzled me as it was not the same Terry I had tolerated over the previous year.

I felt wretched, seeing the hateful, vindictive and judgmental person I truly was. I was no better than the cruel soldiers I had seen during the war. I had not physically harmed anyone, but was my heart any softer than theirs? I could never face Terry again.

Oh, Julia. I had poured my poison onto her, revealing my ugliness. I lay on the grass, heavy sobs wracking my tired old body, frozen by indecision with no path forward. I hated myself, my true self, concealed behind a well-crafted façade. Now it had, without warning, broken through the cracks and spewed forth like a rupturing, infected sore. Amidst soul-wrenching tears, I considered moving far away from these people who loved me. They had seen my façade, which I had always assumed was my true self.

It was getting dark when I hauled my stiff, miserable body off the damp grass and slowly made my way into the house.

I spent the night, with unseeing eyes fixed on the ceiling, searching for a way to rid myself of my stone-cold heart, but found no solution. I thought of self-help programmes, meditation, chanting, and maybe finding a guru. I concluded that I could not change myself, so hopelessness and despair deepened with every passing hour through that dark, frightening, lonely night.

In the morning, 'Call Karen, call Karen', hammered relentlessly in my head, but her religion was the last thing I needed. The words stuck in my head like mud on my boots.

She later said she heard my distress on the phone, although I tried to sound calm, and she knocked on my door within an hour.

CHAPTER TWENTY

Waiting for Karen to arrive, I fussed around straightening cushions and dusting—anything to keep busy and not think of what lay ahead. I hoped I could calmly explain my 'mistake' to Karen, and she could tell me how to smooth things over. I rehearsed the conversation and convinced myself that I would not appear as terrible as I felt. My façade was trying to repair itself, having been shattered the evening before, and I realised that I didn't know how to live without it.

When Karen walked through the door, my plan for a rational conversation with a smooth resolution crumbled. She hugged me, waiting for my tears to subside. When we sat, I trained my eyes on the floor as I explained about the stars on my letterbox and the details of the last few weeks.

'I had written to Terry and also threatened her, Karen.'

Tears flowed like a river bursting through its banks as I recounted the events of the previous day and how I had seen Terry showing kindness to her nasty neighbour. Karen listened patiently, not distracted by the sobs that punctuated my story.

'Karen, I don't understand. Terry has always been the neighbour from Hell. Cold, unkind and always complaining. What is the reason for the sudden change in her? I was positive she was putting those yellow stars on my letterbox. 'Karen understood and confessed that she also had some unpleasant encounters with Terry in the past. She smiled as she assured me there had been a change in Terry, but it was Terry's story to tell. She suggested we go together to see Terry one day soon and allow her to explain.

'She is not well enough for visitors today, as she seemed to have had a setback yesterday,' she added.

Karen didn't need to tell me the cause of it.

I did feel better having told Karen, and to my surprise, Karen did not appear to be shocked. She was as kind to me as on her last visit. Maybe pastor's wives were used to people like me, although I was certain that I, or anyone like me, would be forbidden to cross the threshold of their churches. I never intended to do that, so it didn't bother me. I had to visit Julia, whom I expected to be disgusted with me. The venom she had seen spewing from me appalled me now, and must have had the same effect on her. I didn't have the strength to see her that day, so whether being sensible or afraid, I waited until the following day.

The river broke its banks again when I told Julia what I had seen and what a miserable wretch I was. My closest friend hugged me, saying she understood my anger and forgave me for the outburst.

'I can't accept your forgiveness, Julia, because I don't deserve it, but I hope we can still be friends.'

She laughed and assured me that she had given it anyway and wouldn't love me any less, which I knew to be impossible.

I told Julia that Karen planned to take me to Terry's, and she smiled. I wondered if she knew something that I didn't, but I didn't ask. I would find out for myself.

CHAPTER TWENTY-ONE

I had to wait two uncomfortable days until Karen and I could visit Terry.

Despite the heat of the day, Terry lay on her well-worn couch, with a pillow beneath her head and a colourful quilt for warmth. Jasper sat close beside her, and Terry's long fingers gently stroked her dog's soft ears. Her pale face greeted Karen and me with a warm smile. This was not the Terror who had for the past year delighted in harassing me. That I had considered doing something as cruel as killing Terry's beautiful dog, or even her lovely rose bushes, disgusted me.

I had always considered myself a quiet, easy-going, accommodating lady, but now I had met another Louisa, and I didn't like her at all.

Karen made us each a cup of tea, and we shared the biscuits she had made.

Terry looked into my eyes, saying, 'I am sincerely sorry for how I have treated you, Louisa. I'm so very sorry. I hope and pray that you can forgive me. I want you to know you were not the problem, but it was me.'

I didn't at that time understand what she meant. As far as forgiving her, I didn't know how to do that, so I shrugged. Her smile showed understanding, which I found strange.

Eyes on the ceiling, I said, 'I am sorry about my nasty letter and that I threatened you.'

Smiling, she assured me that she understood my mistake

and did not blame me for thinking she had left the stars.

She replied, 'I would have relished doing something so cruel in the past, Louisa. But the thought disgusts me now.'

I didn't understand what was different now, so I didn't respond.

She then told me about her past. She assured me that she wasn't making excuses for her behaviour, but she wanted me to understand the origins of her attitudes and actions. She said she was raised in a home with loving parents and brothers, but in high school, she was bullied by the girls in her class. It was an all-girls school, and the bullying was relentless. The girls taunted her, stole her things, mocked her and lied about her. She was shunned by all the girls, except by her one friend, who stuck by her throughout her school years. She was treated this way by jealous classmates because she was tall, slim and beautiful. She told us she took no credit for her appearance as it was genetic. She said she looked like her mother and aunt.

Terry said, 'I reported it to the teacher, which made the situation worse. The girls were mildly reprimanded, and that intensified their hatred and mocking. I talked to my parents about it too, but they didn't believe it was as bad as I said, and encouraged me to be friendly to them all.'

Terry explained how good looks can be a disadvantage as it can cause problems. She was talking from more than her own experience, as when she worked in Canberra, she had been encouraged to do some modelling, and there she met models who had suffered because of their looks, some turning to drugs for relief from the pain. People saw them as pretty faces and perfect bodies, not girls with hearts that could be broken.

Wherever Terry went, boys stared at her, but her self-esteem suffered, and she felt worthless and unlovable.

'The final blow came towards the end of my last year when my only friend joined the mockers. She told me she had pretended to be my friend and then stood with the nasty girls and together they all laughed, leaving me alone and humiliated.'

After a pause, Terry added, 'The shock of betrayal was so devastating that I was determined never to trust a girl again. I am ashamed to say, I became boy-crazy and did things in the following years that I deeply regret. I found out the hard way that men could be as heartless as women.'

Terry told us that she was used and abused while searching for love, but concluded that to be used was all she deserved. She tearfully confessed that she had three abortions before she reached the age of twenty-one and experienced numerous betrayals. At university, Terry tried to make friends but found no one she felt she could trust. She resolved to see all women as enemies and never allowed any to get close to her again.

As a result, she built a wall around her heart and became as nasty as those who had rejected and abused her.

She explained that she had spent her life losing herself in books to escape from the real world.

'I joined the book club out of loneliness, although I had no intention of forming any friendships. I love books, and that was the only drawcard.

'I thought God could never forgive me, and I was being punished for my sinful life. I believed a God existed but that He wasn't kind or merciful, so I never prayed or went to a church.'

'No, a kind and merciful God only exists in fairytales,' I said, knowingly.

She raised herself from her pillow, leaning towards me.

'No. No. We have both been wrong, Louisa. Karen has shown me that, and now I have experienced His love and forgiveness.'

I assured her I would not be changing my view. I had seen first-hand how God had allowed the Jews to be massacred during the war.

'Sorry,' I said, 'No. I know the truth. I lived through it.'

At this point, I stood to leave. Terry and Karen asked me to stay and hear the rest of Terry's story, but I had heard enough. If they chose to believe in a loving God, that was their business, but I could not. I told Terry I saw a change in her, and although I didn't understand it, I was happy for her.

'I hope it lasts,' was my parting comment.

At home, I reviewed the conversation, as the forgiveness part played on my mind. I didn't understand how Terry could be so sure she was forgiven. She did not doubt it, and a change had taken place in her that I could not ignore. She was now like Karen, and even Brenda, and a couple of the others I knew who went to the church and all seemed to possess something that I lacked, but I had no idea what it was or how to obtain it.

The mystery I still had not solved was the identity of that boy on the bicycle, and neither Terry, Karen, nor Julia had any ideas.

CHAPTER TWENTY-TWO

The following day, we had our book club meeting, and I hadn't opened the book. I enjoyed the get-together, and I dropped by the library on my way home and picked up our next book. As Julia and Terry had missed the book club, I collected three copies. The book was called *Perplexed* and, without knowing the story, I was sure I could have written it.

Terry came slowly to the door to receive her book and invited me in, but I said my groceries would be arriving soon, so I should go home. It was the truth, but not the reason. I didn't want to hear more talk about God.

My groceries arrived a short time later. I hadn't ordered the mangoes, bread rolls or the BBQ chicken, but I didn't bother calling this time.

Julia came for dinner again.

I wanted to ask her why she had started praying. I'd known her well during the years she lived in Sydney, and back then, she was definitely not what you'd call a "churchy" person. Munching on chicken and salad, she smiled. 'I thought you would be surprised to hear me talk about praying.'

'In the years I knew you before I moved here, I had never been to a church, except a few times as a child. I had been at Christmas and Easter and sometimes with an aunt.'

When John and I moved here, we met Brenda at the cafe, and she was extremely kind to us newcomers. She invited us to church as a way to meet people. We started attending and learnt what Jesus had done for us on the cross. Neither of us had ever heard that before. We had some meetings with the old pastor, the one before David, and he explained to us about repentance and forgiveness. I had some things in my past that I was not proud of, and so did John. The pastor explained that we have all sinned and need God's forgiveness. He shared a lot of things with us and helped us to understand the Bible and the importance of reading it. He was a loving old man and we were sorry when he left, but we have been happy with David, as he is also a good Bible teacher, and lives what he preaches.

'When John became sick four years ago, David and Karen and many of the church people were kind to us. They visited often and prayed for us both. I don't know how I would have made it through the awful time of losing John without the love and support of those dear people. John died peacefully, knowing he was about to see Jesus face-to-face. His death in some strange way was more like a birth than a death, as I felt he was being ushered into a whole new and wonderful world. I am looking forward to being with him again there.'

So, my dearest friend had joined the churchy people. I was happy that she was happy, but was convinced that it wasn't for me.

Handing her a bowl of mango chunks, smothered in cream, I said, 'Hey, please don't expect me to set foot in that place, Julia. That will never happen.'

She smiled and winked at me as she scooped up a spoonful of dessert.

'Seriously, Julia. It will never happen.'

There were some people I needed to avoid for a while, but mostly Karen and Terry. I knew some of the book club ladies attended the church, so I decided to avoid conversations with them, too. I didn't under-stand them, and I was tired of religious talk. As if getting religion and going to a Christian church is the solution to life's problems.

I hadn't played tennis with Irene for three weeks as she

had twisted her ankle badly, supposedly while bushwalking, so I called her and arranged to meet at Common Ground. I insisted on paying for our coffee and lamingtons, despite Brenda's objection.

Irene arrived limping, and it concerned me that her ankle was still painful. A shocking thought flashed through my mind, and the question slipped from my brain and out of my mouth before I could filter it.

'Did Malcolm do this to you?'

'No, no,' she said, a bit too forcefully. I wasn't convinced, but it wasn't any of my business.

We chatted as we sipped our coffee, about tennis and our current book. Our next book was a fantasy novel, a genre I was not familiar with. There were dragons and space flight, intergalactic warriors and the usual hero and a maiden in distress. It was light-hearted enough to be quick to read. Irene said that she found such a far-fetched fantasy a bit annoying, as she preferred books based on reality. I agreed with her, but we both felt it was a worthwhile experience to read a novel like that, and we were interested to hear everyone else's opinion of it.

However, I could think of nothing but that miserable husband of hers, so I asked her if she had called Karen.

She replied, 'I haven't yet, but I intend to soon.'

I dug in my handbag, pulled out the big mobile phone my son insisted I carry, flipped it open and punched in Karen's number. Panic flooded Irene's face as she understood what I was doing.

'Hi, Karen. Louisa here. Yes, yes, I'm fine, but Irene is with me and she needs to speak to you.'

I placed the phone in Irene's shaking hand. She stepped outside, talking softly and came in about ten minutes later. She collapsed into her chair and sighed, 'Thank you.'

CHAPTER TWENTY-THREE

Several days had passed since seeing Karen and Terry, and I became restless. My thoughts were swirling like fallen leaves caught in an autumn breeze. I couldn't concentrate on anything, not even my daily crossword puzzle. I thought about Terry and the change in her, and also about Karen, Brenda and Julia. These people all seemed to have something I lacked, and chuckling to myself, I wondered if perhaps they were aliens.

Despite my determination to keep my distance, I asked Karen to come by to see if I could get a better understanding of what had happened to Terry. She wasn't free to come until the following day. I was disappointed, as I didn't think I could stand this restlessness for another day.

When Karen arrived, we took our coffee onto the front verandah and sat together on my cushioned swing chair, looking out on the beautiful mountains. I confessed my confusion, feeling like a child lost in a blizzard with no sense of direction. I said how peaceful my life had been before the book club started, but now I was being tormented by the haunting name of Dorjan Halmi, and the nightmares had returned. Then the stars appeared.

'Now my predictable, nasty neighbour has been transformed into a person I don't recognise. And I also found out that Julia has joined you lot.'

I told her the hardest thing has been facing my true self.

'I am cold-hearted, cruel, judgmental, and in truth no better than the war criminals in Europe.' I was so ashamed and felt helpless and hopeless, convinced that I could never be any different.

'I have seen the 180 degree change in Terry, where she had gone from nasty to nice, but I don't see how I could ever be capable of changing like she has.'

Karen asked me if I had a Hebrew Bible, and although I was sceptical about what she might say, I reluctantly went looking for my mother's old one. Of course, it was not in English, but in Hungarian.

Maybe now was the time she would hit me with my need to join her church.

As she was flipping through it, I went to the kitchen and made us both a tuna and salad sandwich for lunch and boiled the kettle to make some tea.

I had come to like Karen, so I was concerned that her opening the Bible might mark the end of our friendship.

We chatted about other things while eating our light lunch, and I was hoping she would forget about the Bible, since she would not be able to find what she was looking for, as there was no English in my mother's copy.

However, after we had washed and dried our cups and plates, she picked up the Bible again and asked me if I could translate some passages she had bookmarked, showing God's plan to send Jesus.

'It all started back in the Garden of Eden when God told Satan that a descendant of Eve would crush his head,' she said.

I had never doubted Satan's existence because I had seen his work in Hungary first-hand. She showed me prophecies in my mother's scriptures written even seven hundred years before Jesus' birth, highlighting the details of His birthplace and His time on Earth. It even described His death by crucifixion, written hundreds of years before crucifixion was invented. That got my attention. How did the writers of those ancient books know those things? Was it written by aliens?

Karen went through the Jewish feasts, which she knew better than I did, and showed me how they all pointed to Jesus. I did not doubt that Jesus walked on the earth, as there is more evidence for His life written by non-religious people than there is for famous people like Plato or Caesar. So, the question of Him having ever lived did not bother me, but I doubted He could have been our Messiah. After all, I had heard that He let them kill Him.

Karen then took out her Bible, which had the same books as my mother's, plus twenty-seven more. The first four in the second section, which she said, was called the New Testament, told of Jesus' life, death and resurrection, and the rest of the books were written by various people, including some who had known Jesus while he lived on Earth. Those books explained how we should live. Karen then highlighted for me some things Jesus said and did. He talked a lot about a coming Kingdom, something Jews have been expecting for over four thousand years. I knew little about our religion, but I remember hearing that God promised it to Abraham. But I have only seen Jews being slaughtered like cattle.

No new Kingdom.

Karen also talked to me about God being a father and the immeasurable sacrifice He had made by sending His Son to pay the ransom for our sins. She explained how our sin separated us from God, and how He wanted our relationship to be restored and for Him, the God of the universe, to be a Father to us. Some of the things she told me I had heard from Julia.

'Why did sin need to be paid for?' I asked. 'We can't help doing wrong. We all do it. How could Jesus, if He honestly did, take our place and pay for everyone's sin, anyway?'

Karen answered, 'God is holy and righteous, and He said the wages, or consequence, of sin is death. In the Garden of Eden, He warned Adam and Eve not to disobey Him, or they would die.'

'Well, Karen, from what you have shown me, He was wrong, wasn't He? They didn't die.'

'You are right, Louisa, they didn't fall over dead as you would have expected, but they died in a different way. Their spirits were then separated from God, and He no longer walked and talked with them in the garden. This was more devastating than a physical death. What they lost affected people for over four thousand years.

'Way back then, God already had the plan to send His son Jesus to pay the price for what we had done and restore our relationship with Him. That is how much He loves us, Louisa, and it is far bigger than we can understand.'

Karen explained about the animal sacrifices and the spotless lamb sacrificed each year to pay for the people's sins of the previous year.

'These were a temporary measure showing how Jesus would be the ultimate sacrifice, paying for all our sins, once and for all by shedding His own perfect blood.

'Jesus was the spotless Lamb, the necessary payment for our sins once only, not like the animal sacrifices that had to be repeated each year.'

I wasn't buying it all, as it seemed a bit far-fetched to me. I always saw God, if He even existed, as angry and hateful, and Karen was telling me the opposite. Terry now believed all this, and somehow it had transformed her.

Karen had given me enough to think about for one day, and I realised I had taken up a few hours of her time.When she rose to leave, she said, 'I will leave my Bible here with you, Louisa. I have bookmarked pages you may find helpful.'

I assured her she needn't leave it as I wouldn't touch it, but she insisted.

CHAPTER TWENTY-FOUR

After lunch, I often put my feet up and spend some time reading our next book for the book club meeting. However, when Karen left, I found it almost impossible to tear my gaze from her Bible sitting on the coffee table, as though daring me to pick it up and look inside. I felt a strong magnet pulling me towards it, which I was too weak to resist. I picked up the Bible and settled down to read one or two bookmarked passages, but I continued reading all afternoon and late into the night.

I read a story in the book called John about a lady caught committing adultery. By the law, she should have been stoned, but Jesus forgave her. His kindness was not at all what I expected.

He said if you have seen Him, you know what the Father is like. So, Jesus was saying that God is kind and merciful? That was a foreign concept to me and one I was having difficulty believing. Hadn't He been the one allowing the death of all the Jews in Europe?

I remembered what Karen had said about God paying such an enormous price by sending His son Jesus to pay the price for our sins, just so we could have a relationship with Him again, like Adam and Eve enjoyed.

I also read about the great rabbi, Saul, who had been condoning the murder and imprisonment of Jesus' followers and then became a follower himself. Jesus interrupted his life as he was heading to the capital of Syria to throw more of Jesus' followers into prison. He spent the rest of his life telling everyone about Jesus and suffered terribly for it. Nobody would make such a radical change of direction, unless they were sure. I read how the followers of Jesus, including His mother, had been transformed during the Feast of Pentecost. Peter bravely told the people they had killed the Messiah. They asked what they should do, and he told them to repent and be baptised. Three thousand of them did that same day, and more believed each day after that. I had always believed in hell, and now I knew I probably would be heading there.

I had a strong desire to do something to save myself, as it seemed that Jesus was the answer. Cleansing and forgiveness up until this point had seemed impossible, but now I hoped I could experience it. I called Karen the next morning and asked for her help. I shared what I had read and how Jesus' kindness, mercy and love amazed me.

'I need Jesus's forgiveness, Karen, but I don't understand how to get it. I am not sure I can give up control of my life. Maybe I am too old anyway. Do I have to go to church? How can I remember everything I have done wrong? Are you sure this is available to everyone?'

I fired all these questions at her as soon as she picked up the phone. She laughed, saying she could be at my house in an hour or two.

I sat down to read again, but was interrupted by Bessie bellowing near the fence. I had forgotten to milk her! Not once in all the years I had her did I ever forget to milk her first thing in the morning. Gypsy and Mango were serpentining in and out of my legs, wondering where their food was also. What was happening to me?

By the time I finished my chores and remembered to feed myself, Karen arrived.

CHAPTER TWENTY-FIVE

When I opened the door, Karen didn't step inside, as she had arranged with Terry for us to visit her. I hadn't seen Terry since I walked out of her place the previous week, uninterested in the rest of her story. I didn't know how she had reacted to my sudden departure, so I felt a bit nervous, like a kid who had failed a test and was unsure of her parents' reaction. I had no choice but to go, as I sensed Karen wasn't about to accept a refusal.

Terry's health had improved, as she now sat comfortably in one of her black leather recliners. She smiled warmly, which gave me courage, enabling me to tackle the issue head-on.

'What happened to you, Terry?'

She smiled at me and looked fondly towards Karen.

'I have Karen to thank for what I have experienced,' she said.

She explained how Karen had come to visit her for several months before the book club started and had encouraged her to join, knowing her love of books and also her loneliness.

Karen's earlier visits had not been pleasant, as Terry had been rude to her and told her not to come back. But Karen kept visiting and each time brought a small gift like a card, a flower, or chocolate.

'A part of me looked forward to her visits, and another part didn't want her to come. I had determined not to get myself into a position where I could be hurt again.'

Bit by bit, Karen broke down Terry's carefully constructed

wall. She was convinced the safest way to protect herself was to be cold and rude. However, Karen persisted, despite Terry's cold reception.

Terry said, 'I suspected Karen might be different from other women and I cautiously allowed her to peer through the cracks that were developing in my wall.'

Then came the day when the dam burst. A flood of emotion gushed out as the wall came down. With tears, Terry told Karen the betrayals and cruelty she had endured at school and university. I had heard this on my last visit, and when they began to talk about God, I had left. Now I was interested to hear that part of her story.

Terry's eyes were alive as she launched into the next chapters.

The day Terry's emotional floodgates burst, she asked Karen why she kept returning and enduring her nasty reception.

'Karen told me that she loved me, cared about me and understood my pain. Karen explained how Jesus offered to wipe away my hurt and pain through repentance and forgiveness.'

Terry said she had laughed, telling Karen that was something for storybooks, and not at all possible.

Karen explained how Jesus had paid the price with His life for all the pain and heartache this life could deliver.

Terry said, 'At this point, I had stopped Karen, saying I knew I could never be forgiven for killing three babies. Karen told me that Jesus laid down His life for us and offered us forgiveness and the ability to 'start again' — be born again, she called it.'

As Terry continued talking, I began to understand some things Karen and Julia had both told me.

'I had hoped there was a way I could break free from the pain and guilt I lived with, and Karen assured me it was possible,' Terry added.

Terry described the journey that brought her to accept what Jesus had done for her through His death and resurrection.

'With Karen's explanation and my study of the Scriptures, I

realised my need for a saviour and my strong desire to be forgiven for my sins. I wanted to commit myself to serve and love Jesus, and come to know God as my Heavenly Father.'

Karen then said, 'The Creator of the universe wants to have a personal relationship with each of us. He suffered the agony of watching His Beloved Son pay the price for our sin, which was a much greater act of love than we mere humans can ever fully understand. Yet, He has called us to be the recipients of that love and enjoy a close relationship with Him.'

Terry added, 'Once convinced of these truths, I could not wait another minute to declare my gratitude and to yield my life into those loving hands. I asked the Father to please forgive me of a number of things that came instantly to my mind, and accept me into His family.'

She told me of the peace and joy that then filled her. She knew without a doubt that He had heard her simple prayer and that He had forgiven her.

'At that moment, I understood what Karen had been telling me about being born again. I experienced a fresh start, and I felt clean. Karen explained that when we give our lives to Jesus in repentance, our spirit, which had been dormant, comes alive.'

Terry added, 'There is a verse in the Bible that says as far as the east is from the west is how far He will remove our sins from us when we repent. There is no further distance in the universe.'

Hearing all this and having the evidence of a changed life sitting in front of me, both excited and scared me. It reminded me of the first time I had stood on a high diving board and had wanted very much to jump, but at the same time was too scared to move.

Karen took over the conversation and shared her own story, which she had recently shared with Terry. What I heard next was almost unbelievable.

CHAPTER TWENTY- SIX

Karen's father and mother were both alcoholics. She was the oldest of five children who occasionally attended school, often arriving hungry and dirty. She had to look after her younger brothers and sisters, as often neither parent came home at night. One evening, a stranger came to the door, accompanied by two police officers. They told Karen that her parents were in gaol and that the children were all going to foster care. Neighbours were concerned for the children and had notified the authorities numerous times about the conditions in which they were living. As a girl of twelve, Karen was devastated and terrified, even though the police officers and the social worker were kind and gentle. They looked at the disgusting conditions the children were living in, and to Karen's surprise, one of the police officers was crying. He told her he was a daddy and could not bear to think of his children or any child having to live like this.

Karen explained, 'His kindness was so foreign to me that when he reached out to touch me, I screamed and kicked him and tried to bite him.'

The skinny, frightened children were taken to the local hospital. The staff found them unmanageable, so they kept them together but separate from the other patients.

After some days, they were taken to the foster home of a man and a woman, James and Sally, who had no children. All five of them were able to stay together, something Karen later learned was unusual.

She explained with a smile, 'This poor couple had a gigantic job ahead of them. We didn't even know how to use a knife and fork, and had no idea of hygiene or manners. Looking back on those days, years later, I remember how we behaved, and we were all pretty wild and uncontrollable.'

Apart from these challenges, all five of them were angry, hurting children who were unfamiliar with kindness.

'We tested that couple at every opportunity, waiting for James and Sally to turn on us and kick us out, or at least beat us.'

Gradually, their new mum and dad began to see the fruit of their labour. The children took time to trust them, eventually allowing themselves to be touched and later hugged. For Karen, this took some months.

My mouth was gaping as Karen continued talking. I could not believe she was talking about her own childhood. She smiled, knowing what I was thinking.

'My adopted mum and dad were, and still are, the most Christlike people I have ever met. Through all the turmoil, mistrust, and violence, they demonstrated the love of Jesus.

'The patience they had with us was so strange, as we were used to anger and violence. We used to get hit by our parents for nothing, so I remember thinking I might as well be naughty as I was going to get hit anyway. But our new mum and dad were kind to us, no matter how naughty we were. I would tempt them to get angry by being as rude and nasty as I could, but their patience never ran out.

'Mum used to often say as she held me, "This is not who you are, Karen. You are a good girl and can behave well. You are going to grow up to be a wonderful woman, and someday you may be a wife to a wonderful man and a mother to some beautiful children."

'Eventually, I started to absorb what she had been saying and tried hard to be the person she believed me to be.

'They both told us stories about Jesus, and over time our mockery turned to interest and ultimately to accepting Jesus as our Saviour and Healer. As a result of their love and teaching, we are all now followers of Jesus. None of us has been tempted to follow the path of our biological parents.'

I asked Karen if I could meet her wonderful parents, and she said they lived in a town two hours from us and she would organise for them to visit. She suggested we could have lunch together the following week.

I didn't think they could be real.

CHAPTER TWENTY-SEVEN

When I met James and Sally, I was surprised at how young they were, and when I commented, they explained.

'We were in our early twenties when we took in Karen and her brothers and sisters.'

They had been married for about a year when they felt that the Lord had told them that they would not have children of their own, but were to raise someone else's family. They had wondered if perhaps a relative might die and leave a family of sweet children.

'When we had a visit from a Christian friend who worked in foster care, we were surprised, as this wasn't an avenue that we had considered. She described the condition in which the children were found, and explained they were in the local hospital waiting to be placed in foster care.'

Their friend had said, 'We need someone urgently to take these children. No one wants to take on five disturbed children, but we think it will traumatise the children further to split them up.'

The friend told Sally and James that she couldn't stop thinking about them, wondering if they were the Lord's solution for these children. She added that she didn't want them to feel pressured, as the Lord promised to provide for the children. The foster organisation was run by Christians who prayed for the children in their care, especially for their placement.

James said, 'We both knew this was the Lord's plan for us,

even though it wasn't what we had envisaged.'

After a short time talking together, with peace in their hearts, they told their friend they wanted to take them all, not as foster children, but with the view of adopting them. The necessary paperwork and home checks were expedited so the children could move in without further delay.

Karen's mother smiled warmly at her and added, 'So we took in five crazy kids.'

Both of her parents spent their time over lunch explaining how they could not have raised the children without the Lord. They leaned on Him daily for patience, strength and wisdom and even for His love for the children.

They described the early weeks. 'We couldn't leave the house or have anyone visit as the children were so wild. They grabbed food with their hands as if no more food would ever be offered to them. They snatched from each other, although plenty was available for them all. It broke our hearts to see it. They had no idea about sleeping all night or sleeping in separate beds. They had not attended school for quite some time, so even Karen couldn't read or write. Showering properly and washing their hands were also things they had to be taught.'

They read stories to the children and, as they had no books in their former 'home', they were fascinated by the stories and pictures.

Sally said, 'I made the mistake once of leaving a book on a chair when I left the room and came back to find pages had been ripped out and the book thrown across the room.'

I looked at Karen in amazement, and she smiled.

She explained, 'Later, I could look back on my life and understand why I destroyed things I liked, and was so cruel to my parents. I felt certain the nice things and the loving people would soon be gone, so it was better to take control and get rid of them first to protect myself from the hurt I believed would come. I expected the love and kindness to end, and my brothers and sisters and I would be sent back to the house we had come from.'

Months passed before they saw much change in the children. The youngest, still in nappies, was the first to accept affection. They remarked that Karen proved the hardest to reach.

Karen explained, 'It took me a considerable time to begin to trust them. One thing that I both liked and hated was the stories they always told us about Jesus. Nobody could love like that, and yet this mum and dad,' she added beaming as she wrapped an arm around each of them, 'were like the Jesus they talked about and seemed to know and love.'

Sally said that through all this, family members and friends were praying for the children. About a month after the children arrived, they took them to their church but stayed for just two songs. They allowed the children to take their time to get used to the people and the unfamiliar environment.

Sally said, 'Karen kept hiding her new clothes and it took me a while to realise why she was doing it.'

Karen smiled. 'I had never owned pretty clothes, so I feared they would be taken away from me.'

I spent an interesting hour hearing about the transformation of each of the children, and James and Sally gave all the praise and glory to God. I tried to congratulate them on doing such an amazing job, but they refused to take any credit, assuring me that Jesus did it all.

Each child had fears, hurts and memories, and Karen's parents had to learn to deal with each in unique ways. They have all come to put their faith in Jesus, and He has continued the transforming work in each of their lives.

James said, 'These children became, and still are, the biggest blessings in our lives, far above what we ever dreamed possible. The Lord blessed us with five of His treasures.'

This story had a great impact on me as Jesus seemed so real and actively involved in their lives. This could not have happened to these children by chance, or even as a result of excellent parenting. They said the children had not just improved in behaviour, but that they were radically changed. Like Terry, each one of these children had been born again by the power of God.

I felt sure I should take some action, but I was hesitant. It seemed like a big step to take, and if I did take it, my life would also change as I would no longer be my own boss.

I decided to discuss this with someone not churchy, and my new friend Rosa was my obvious choice.

I invited Rosa for lunch the following day, saying that I had some things to share with her and I wanted to ask her advice.

CHAPTER TWENTY-EIGHT

When Rosa arrived, I wrapped her in a hug. I hadn't seen her for several days as she had been interstate.

When we settled down to eat the egg and spinach pie and the salad I had prepared, she smiled and asked, 'What's going on, Louisa? I have been away just a short while, and I feel I must have missed something.'

I didn't often share my thoughts and feelings, but I felt comfortable talking with Rosa. During our times together, she shared her pain and loss with me, and it was now my turn.

She had read my letter but knew nothing about the yellow stars. I told her about the times the stars appeared on my letter-box. Rosa was horrified that someone would do such a thing and understood the pain it had caused.

'Did you find out who was putting them there?'

'No, I haven't yet.'

I said I had accused Terry and had threatened and abused her. Shame and regret surfaced again as I told Rosa how I had behaved.

Rosa laughed, saying, 'I can't imagine you storming over to Terry's house and threatening her.'

I cringed and told her I discovered that it had not been Terry, and how I had seen her remove one, hoping I hadn't seen it there. Rosa's jaw dropped.

'You mean our Terry was doing something kind? I find that hard to imagine.'

'I had the same reaction, Rosa. Terry has changed and become religious, which leaves me confused.'

'She is sweet and kind and even said she forgave me for being angry with her.

'It sounds strange, but I have seen it myself. She talks about God being loving and how He has forgiven her sins and changed her heart.

'I want to hear your opinion on all this, Rosa, because I know you are well-educated and wise. Do you think such a change is possible? Karen also has a story of her life being changed and healed. I have never heard anything like this before. They both talk about a righteous God, being born again and having their sins washed away.'

I waited for a response from Rosa, but she lowered her eyes and said nothing.

We sat in silence for a while until she muttered, 'I once believed all that stuff.'

Looking at me, she added, 'Until God killed my husband and baby. Then I knew I had believed a lie. How can they say we have a kind and loving God, when He hurts us so much?'

Her question was one I couldn't answer and it was one that had bothered me as well. I knew there must be an answer and I was determined to find it, not just for Rosa but for myself also.

I had heard people say God is in control, which never made sense to me. It looked as though he had certainly lost control in Europe in the 1940's. There was daily evidence of His lack of control. Why did he let Andrew die like that? What about Julia's husband, John and Rosa's husband too, of course? Why do innocent children suffer? Karen told me that God wants everyone to be saved. So why doesn't He save everyone?

I could see I had upset her, so I changed the subject, as I had no answer to her question, but was determined to see what I could find out before I saw her again. We chatted about other things, including the latest book for the book club, but Rosa remained uncomfortable. I thought she was worried I was getting sucked into a false religion.

I suspected Rosa must be wrong to see God that way, but I didn't know why. I understood that God sent Jesus as an amazing act of love to draw us into a relationship with Him. At this point, that was the most important thing I understood.

I knew I had to take action based on my understanding, although I still didn't have an answer for Rosa.

She left soon after lunch and said she would see me again in a week or so, as she was going away the following day and would miss our book club meeting again.

CHAPTER TWENTY-NINE

Karen and I visited Terry again as Terry's health had improved. Karen explained to me that following Jesus is a relationship, not obeying a set of rules, like other religions. I remembered how I had read in her Bible about Jesus' love and the authority with which He spoke and how lives were transformed by both His power and His compassion. I didn't think these two characteristics could belong together in one person. The people I had seen with power used it for their ends, at the expense of everyone else. I had come to the same place as Terry, knowing that I needed to be saved and transformed by Jesus, with no doubt in my mind that Jesus was real and alive and that I needed Him.

The question I then had was, 'What must I do to know Jesus and be saved?'

Karen showed me the book of Romans in the New Testament, which says, "Whoever will call upon the name of the LORD will be saved."

Karen and Terry both then explained to me about repentance. I had heard the word and seen it in Karen's Bible. Peter had told the crowd at Pentecost to repent and be baptised. Terry said repentance is asking forgiveness for the things we have done, and even thoughts that displease the Lord.

I panicked. 'How can I remember them all since I have had over sixty years of sinning?' They told me to ask forgiveness for the things I could remember, and that repentance is not a one-time event, but we go on repenting throughout our lives of things from the past that the Lord brings to mind, as well as the thoughts, words or actions that displease Him in our daily lives. Repentance goes beyond being sorry and asking for forgiveness, but also means doing the opposite of what you had been doing.

Karen said, 'Ephesians Chapter 4 explains how we should live. It says if you used to steal, don't just stop stealing, but start giving. If you have cursed people, don't just stop cursing but start blessing people instead.

It would take some time to understand all these things, but I needed to repent and make Jesus my Lord and my Saviour. I understood that Jesus was our Jewish Messiah, whom we had been waiting for over four thousand years. Yet when He came, I wondered why my forefathers didn't recognise Him. Karen explained that He didn't come as the conquering king they were expecting, although a large number of Jews did believe Jesus was their Messiah, with over three thousand believing in one day. They didn't understand that He would be coming twice. First, as the suffering servant paying the price for the sins of the world and defeating Satan, and the second time as the King of Kings and the Righteous Judge. I asked Karen and Terry when He came the second time, and Karen explained that He had not yet come as the Judge but would return soon.

I didn't want to wait any longer and asked them both to help me accept that Jesus had paid for my sin and show me how to make Him the Lord of my life. The three of us knelt on Terry's carpet, and Terry asked me to talk to Him.

As soon as I whispered, 'Dear Jesus,' the tears broke loose. Between sobs, I asked Jesus to forgive my sins, mentioning the ones that came to mind, including my past hatred of Terry. She was sniffing now, too. I asked Jesus to be my Saviour and told Him I would try to be obedient. Saying these words and meaning them had a profound effect on my heart. I was flooded with love and peace, and I felt Jesus was present with me. My tears turned to laughter and then back to tears, and then both flowed together. I had never experienced such a wonderful feeling. Terry cried while Karen laughed. I hugged Terry and then stopped and confessed, 'Several months ago, I changed your name from "Terry" to "Terror". Today I think I will change it from Terror to Teary.'

The three of us hugged, laughed, hugged, and cried until we all collapsed on our chairs. Oh, what joy. Oh, what healing. Oh, what love.

I left Terry's house overflowing with joy and feeling that my life had started afresh. The sun was shining brighter, the birds were singing joyfully, and the colours of the flowers were richer than ever. I was grateful that this change was possible for me, even at my age. Karen had come to know Jesus as a child, and I as an older lady. Late in life far outweighs never. I was and am extremely thankful that Jesus led me to people who introduced Him to me, and now I want to tell everyone about Him.

However, I still needed to take another important step.

CHAPTER THIRTY

The next day, Karen gifted me with a Bible, and I couldn't wait to read it. I had, of course, never owned one and had never read my mother's Hungarian Jewish Bible. I don't think my mother had either. Karen recommended I start with a Gospel, found at the beginning of the New Testament. She suggested Matthew as it was written by a Jew, as she thought I would be familiar with the customs. I think she was more familiar with them than I was, as my family for generations had not been practicing Jews.

The Gospels, the first four books, talk about what Jesus did and taught while He was here on earth. She asked me to read the book called The Acts of the Apostles next, which is the book after the four Gospels and describes what the disciples did after Jesus returned to Heaven.

I took two days to read through Matthew and then started on Acts. I didn't touch our book for the book club that week, even though Julia had told me it was a funny book. I felt reading the Bible was more important at this stage. I had a sense of urgency to learn about Jesus and how we should live this life.

When I read how the disciples told people they needed to get baptised, I was convinced that I should also. I checked with Karen, and she agreed.

'Why didn't you tell me two days ago?'

'We wanted you to request it yourself, rather than doing it because we told you to. We wanted it to come from you, being led by the Holy Spirit.'

I was amazed and encouraged to see that Jesus was already

leading and guiding me.

'Where, Karen? And when?'

'As soon as possible and where there is enough water,' she said.

'Enough water?' I asked. 'John the Baptist baptised people in a river, but I have seen in movies that babies get a bit of water sprinkled on their heads. Isn't that enough?'

I had heard that baptism, or christening as some people call it, was a ceremony where babies got water sprinkled on them and the minister or priest prayed, but I couldn't find that in my Bible. The Bible says we must first repent and then be baptised. Karen said it was never meant to be something for babies, but that was a tradition started about 300 AD, which was never done by Jesus or the disciples.

They had some sort of a tub at the church, but I wasn't going there. Despite what had happened to me, I told Karen I didn't want to go to her church. She understood and explained that baptism doesn't have to happen in a church building. She said that baptism is dying to our old life and rising out of the water into the new life in Christ, and all we need is enough water.

'You can't do that with a bit of water sprinkled on your head, and definitely not as a baby. Little babies can't repent, and that is necessary before baptism. If Jesus did it by being fully immersed in the water, we should follow his example.'

She said it is not symbolic, but a spiritual experience. Sometimes, addictions simply fall away, and many are left feeling clean, thoroughly washed and filled with joy. There is no right or wrong feeling at baptism, but she explained that if you go into the water unrepentant, nothing happens except you get wet. After repenting, some people get filled with the Holy Spirit at their baptism, the same Spirit that filled a crowd of people at the feast of Pentecost.

I was excited about my baptism, but asked Karen if she thought I was good enough. I wondered if I had to pass a test or be a better person before I could be baptised. She told me some people think that, but that is not what the Bible says. The important prerequisite in the Bible is repentance. She told me about Philip, one of Jesus' disciples, who shared the gospel with a man riding in a carriage. When the man understood what Jesus had done for him, they stopped the carriage near some water, and he was baptised immediately.

I was excited about my baptism now, but I had a problem.

'Karen, I can't swim.'

She assured me it did not matter, as she'd be in the water with me, the water wouldn't be deep, and we would find a suitable place.

We chose a quiet spot along Wattle Creek, a short distance from town. The weather was warm, and I hoped the water would be too. I was determined to do it anyway to please Jesus, knowing what He had done for me. I asked Julia and Terry about their baptisms, and both had different experiences.

Julia was baptised several years ago when the old pastor was still in Wattle Creek. She and her husband, John, were baptised at the same time in the church building, when they decided to give their lives to Jesus. She remembered it as a joyful time, and although she didn't feel any difference, she was glad she did it. She knew it was significant spiritually, as our enemy does not like us to take that step of total consecration to Jesus.

Terry had a dramatic experience at her baptism, a month before mine. She had felt a battle going on inside her mind and body. She called Karen three times to say she could not do it, and each time called her back, saying she would be there. She thought she was going crazy as she was terrified, but she knew it was an important and necessary step. She went to the church, but she started crying and shaking when she looked at the water, and couldn't go close to it. Karen and David understood there was a spiritual battle going on and that the enemy did not want her to be baptised. They prayed with her, and she was then able to step into the water. As soon as her head came out of the water, she felt a wave of peace and joy flood over her. She repeated, 'I am free, I am free!' She laughed as she recounted the day, saying her pain was washed away in the water, although she didn't understand how. She just knew Jesus had washed her and set her free.

And now it was my turn. I wanted my special friends to be there - Karen, Julia and my previously obnoxious neighbour, Terry. I also wanted to invite Rosa, but remembered that she was still away.

We went to the creek on a Tuesday afternoon, knowing it was unlikely that we would see other people there at that time of day. I wore a faded gardening T-shirt, worn-out cotton slacks and took some towels. I was still nervous about the water, but Karen reassured me it was not deep. Julia and Terry hugged me with knowing smiles as I stepped cautiously into the cool water, where Karen took my hand. The water was clear enough to see the stones and the sand on the bottom as I gingerly waded into the creek. Karen stopped where the water was up to her waist and showed me how to hold my nose. She put one arm around me, declaring, 'I baptise you in the Name of the Father, Son and Holy Spirit'. I closed my eyes and felt my ears fill with water as Karen lowered me under. As she lifted me up, I let out a shout, taking us all by surprise as joy bubbled up inside me. I had read a verse about our sins being like scarlet, but how Jesus washes them as white as snow.

My friends laughed as I exclaimed, 'I'm clean, I'm clean.' Hugging, two wet and two dry ladies soon became four wet sisters. I was sure I would never stop smiling.

We all went to my house to pray and praise the Lord together. Julia, Karen and Terry all laid their hands on me and asked the Lord to fill me with His Holy Spirit. I did not expect to feel anything, but I felt like a bolt of electricity passed through me. It made me jump.

'What just happened to me? I told them what I felt.

Karen said, 'It sounds as though you just received the answer to our prayer, but there is no formula to what you should experience. Some people feel nothing, and some laugh, cry, yell or even see a vision. It is up to the Lord, as He is the giver. Some immediately speak in tongues, and some may start speaking in tongues at another time, perhaps when they least expect it.

As we sat drinking steaming tea, after Karen and I had showered, I asked Karen, 'Now, what are the rules I need to keep? Can you give me the list? I know the Ten Commandments, but I am sure there are more.

CHAPTER THIRTY-ONE

Karen was surprised by my question. She smiled and explained that we are no longer under the Old Covenant that God gave to Moses, which required the shedding of the blood of goats and cows. We are under a new covenant instituted by Jesus shedding His own precious blood as a one-time final sacrifice.

Joking, I said, 'Good. Because you are not getting my Bessie for a sacrifice. So, what are the rules now, Karen?'

'Under this New Covenant, we have the rules written on our hearts. That means that now we belong to Jesus, and the Holy Spirit will teach us what is right and wrong. As we read the Bible, God's Word to us, we learn how we should live.

'A clear explanation is found in John 15.'

I picked up my Bible, and Karen asked me to read it aloud.

After reading the description of Jesus being like a vine and us being the branches, I could understand the importance of staying connected to Jesus, our vine.

'I understand about grape vines. I have one out the back which I need to prune right back in the winter so it will produce good fruit. I notice, too, that if a branch is disconnected from the vine, it dies quickly. Even any fruit that may be on it withers up and dies.'

Karen said, 'You understand then what Jesus is saying here about how important it is for us to stay connected to Him at all times in order to learn and grow.'

'Yes, and I see that the fruit is not for us but for the Father, the vinedresser. '

I laughed, adding, 'I am the vinedresser of my little grapevine and the fruit is for me.'

Terry said she couldn't read her Bible and pray all day because she had things she needed to do. She didn't understand how we could stay connected when we were busy.

Karen explained that we shouldn't separate our lives into times with the Lord and times doing "unspiritual" things, but we can do everything with Him.

'Look up Colossians 3:17.'

I opened my New American Standard Bible again, and Julia helped me to find Colossians, a book I hadn't read.

"And whatever you do in word or deed, do all in the name of the Lord Jesus, giving thanks through Him to God the Father."

Karen added, 'This wonderful life we have in Christ is about a relationship with our heavenly Father made possible by Jesus paying the penalty necessary for our sins. It is a marvellous privilege that the Old Testament prophets could only glimpse from afar.

'Louisa, you would understand about the temple rituals. You know about the Holy of Holies where God dwelt. Just one person, a priest, was allowed to go in there, behind the curtain, once a year. Do you know the first thing that God did when Jesus died?'

I had no idea and couldn't even come up with a good guess. Terry couldn't think of the answer either.

'God Himself ripped that enormous, thick curtain from top to bottom. From that moment on, we all have had access to the presence of the Father, instead of just one priest being allowed to go in once a year. Those priests used to have to do all sorts of cleansing rituals and sacrifices to enter God's presence behind that curtain. If he wasn't properly prepared before he went in, he would die. Now we have that access because of the blood of Jesus. What a privilege.

'The New Covenant Jesus instituted by His death is for a relationship instead of rules, and causes us to want to please Him in all we do. He has called us to live holy lives, and Jesus enables us to do that by filling us with His Holy Spirit.

'Whether reading our Bibles or washing our dishes, or any task, driving or resting, or even milking your cow, Louisa, we now do everything with Jesus.'

We talked further about this wonderful life in which we are never alone. What a privilege to live moment by moment with the King of Kings.

We all washed the cups and plates, laughing, remembering Jesus was in the midst of us while doing something menial, and I loved it.

The Lord had something quite unexpected for me the following day.

CHAPTER THIRTY-TWO

The day after my baptism, I heard a faint knocking on my front door soon after milking Bessie. It was unusual that someone would drop by so early. Charlotte, who was a member of the book club, was standing on my front verandah, agitated and nervous. I couldn't imagine what had happened to her, or why she had come to see me. I wondered if she needed some help from Karen, rather than me.

I had spoken with Charlotte several times at book club and had bumped into her at the cafe and had coffee with her, but I didn't know her well.

She is a lot younger than I, in her early 40s, and is very busy with her children. She is Rosa's younger sister.

Recently, we read a book titled *House Trained Worms*, which was the tale of a single mum who had seven children with diverse personalities and needs. The hilarious book had some of us remembering the antics of our own children and relating to the mother's challenges.

Charlotte had said the book resembled her real life. She is an active, beautiful woman who seems to attack life's challenges with confidence. The book club for her is a welcome reprieve from her hectic and challenging home life. She had shared little at our first meeting except the names and ages of her five children, and that she is raising them on her own.

However, as we discussed this book, she talked about her concerns for her 16-year-old son Jason, who was mixing with the wrong crowd at school.

I remembered her sharing about him at that meeting, but still couldn't think of a reason for her to come and visit this old lady.

She apologised for coming by early, but she had just dropped the children at school and thought if she didn't come straight away, she might talk herself out of coming at all. I was confused with no idea what she was worried about.

To my great surprise, she started crying when we sat together on the swing chair, holding our mugs of coffee. I waited for her to compose herself while scrambling to think of a reason why she would be sad and why she would feel nervous about coming to see me.

She took a breath, and mustering some courage, she began.

'At book club, Terry mentioned the stars on your mailbox, saying she had seen a boy delivering them,' she whispered. She was wringing her hands as though trying to untangle her fingers while working on her courage. Overwhelmed with heartache and shame, her words tumbled out, 'It was my son.'

Charlotte's shaking hands and shifting eyes showed her fear of my response. She anticipated an angry reaction from me, assuming that I would punish her son and chastise her for having such a cruel boy.

She hurried on, reminded me that she had misplaced her copy of my letter, and came across it when tidying one of her son's rooms. She also found yellow cardboard, which he must have taken from school, and a plastic star-shaped template. She was shocked and didn't know what to do. She knew she had to come and tell me so I could punish him.

She felt a failure as a mother since one of her children did something so mean.

'I will leave the book club, as I expect I will no longer be welcome after you tell the ladies what my son has done.'

It was then that I knew a dramatic change had taken place in me. I recollected how I had wanted to make Terry suffer for her supposed crime. I was ashamed, realising dear Charlotte was expecting me to pour the same venom onto her and her son.

I wrapped my arms around her and held her. My tears also came, but for another reason. My heart filled with love for Charlotte and her son and with shame for my previous reaction. I had experienced amazing forgiveness, so how could I not forgive this distraught mother and her boy, who was trying to make his way in the world without the love and support of his dad?

With my arm around her shoulder, I said, 'Firstly, I don't blame you for your son's actions, and secondly, this solution to the mysterious stars is a secret between us. I doubt anyone in the book club has even seen the stars.'

'Oh yes,' she said. 'Everyone has been talking about them, wondering who would do such a thing to you.'

I was reminded once again of the kindness of the ladies in our book club. No one had spoken to me about the stars. I wanted to meet her son as soon as possible and tell him I had forgiven him. She had told him that she was coming to see me, and he was angry and afraid, certain I had called the police.

'Please assure him that I have no intention of calling the police. However, I would like to meet him and have a chat.

'Do you think you could persuade him to come and see me? I know it would be a hard thing for him to do, but I want him to see that I have forgiven him.'

We both felt it was important for him to come and apologise, even though it would be difficult.

'I will send him around after school today. The sooner the better, I think. I know he is terrified of the consequences and asked me if he would be going to gaol. Honestly, I did not expect your forgiveness or your kindness to me. I will tell him how kind you have been and encourage him to come.'

Charlotte then shared how her husband had left her for a younger woman. He had continued to be generous in child support, but not in the support his children craved. She said they were all suffering in different ways. Jason had been a happy kid until his dad left, and now he is moody and disobedient. Her oldest daughter, Anna, who is just a bit older than Jason, is sullen and uncooperative. Charlotte's life was an exhausting challenge every day, and the book club was an enjoyable break from her usual routine. It was the one activity all week that was for her pleasure alone.

I saw how selfish my life had been, focused on my happiness — my garden, my pets and my quiet life. Despite brief glimpses of my friends' struggles, I had never considered offering my help. I thought of Charlotte and her children, Terry and her continuing health problems, Irene and her challenging marriage, Brenda with the responsibility of running the café, Rosa living alone, as well as the struggles of some of the other ladies. I had a great opportunity to help these ladies and was dismayed at my self-centredness.

Charlotte left an hour later, feeling lighter than when she had arrived. I was looking forward to 16-year-old Jason coming to see me.

Later that afternoon, a lanky teenager with curly blond hair hanging in his eyes sauntered toward my front door, hunched shoulders, hands deep in his jeans pockets and head hanging low.

CHAPTER THIRTY-THREE

I opened the door to a young man armed with his excuses.

I smiled and offered him a seat on the verandah. He slouched in my rickety cane chair, re-tying his perfectly tied sneakers. I jumped in, telling him I had seen him place a star and ride away. As he opened his mouth to speak, I leaned forward and touched his arm. I told him I forgave him, and his prepared excuses vaporised. He mumbled that he didn't mean any harm, that it was a stupid prank, and still looking at his shoes, he said he was sorry. He had told the idea to one of the popular kids at school who had dared him, in front of the rest of the class, to do it. He didn't want to, but felt he would never hear the end of it if he backed down.

'It was such a dumb, stupid idea,' he said, 'and I shouldn't have done it.

'I would often hang around and watch what happened. Sometimes I saw you take it down, or another lady take it down. I even saw a man take it down a few times. Sometimes the stars would stay there 'til the next day, especially if I put them up late in the day, but they would usually disappear the same day I put them there.

'Every day they asked me at school if I have put up another one, as I told them that someone always took them down. If I said "yes", they all cheered. I felt a mixture of joy from being popular and disgust at what I was doing.'

His tear-filled eyes scanned every direction but mine. I invited him inside for a drink to break the awkward silence, and he reluctantly followed me into the kitchen. I took some lemonade and ice from the fridge, filled two tall glasses and opened a packet of biscuits. We sat on the bar stools at the kitchen counter and drank the cold lemonade while Jason munched on some biscuits. To break the awkward silence, I asked him about school, trying to get to know him and help him relax, but his answers were short, as though he was anxious to leave. I talked to him about the dangers of peer pressure, although I knew he was well aware of the effect it had on him.

But when he gazed out the window and saw Bessie, his countenance changed.

'You have a cow?? A Jersey? I love cows. I'm going to be a farmer. Can I go and pat her? Do you milk her? I have never milked a cow.'

'Would you like to learn how to milk her?' I asked.

'Could I?' He answered, his eyes suddenly alive.

I immediately had an idea and told him to come at 6:30 on Saturday, and we could milk her together, and I would also show him how I separate the milk and cream. I suggested that we could then make blueberry pancakes, adding that he could put as much cream on them as he wanted.

He resembled a child on Christmas morning, and I instantly loved that boy. We talked for quite a while as he explained to me his dream of becoming a farmer. Now that his dad was gone, he had no one to teach him farming, but he would be pleased if he could learn to milk my cow. It was high on his list of things he wanted to learn. He said he was interested in sheep as well as cows, and was borrowing books from the library to learn all he could. He was chatty and relaxed when we were talking about farming. I told him I had a cow when I was younger than him, when I lived in Hungary, but we didn't have sheep. I told him we had a few goats. He asked me questions about raising goats, but I confessed I couldn't tell him much as I didn't like our goats.

'Bucks smell terrible,' I said. He thought that was pretty

funny.

After he finished his lemonade and some biscuits, I took him to meet Bessie and the chickens. He patted Gypsy and Mango and chatted to them as they followed us into the yard.

He mentioned that he didn't have any grandmas but that I reminded him of what he thought it would be like to have one.

I stood on the verandah an hour later, after I had answered several questions about Bessie and Jersey cows in general, watching him as he headed towards his bike.

With a bounce in his step and a cheeky grin, he turned to me, saying, 'See you on Saturday, Grandma.'

As I laughed and waved, my heart was full.

'Thank you, Lord. Thank you for what you have done in me, and for what You are going to do in that boy,' I whispered.

CHAPTER THIRTY-FOUR

Rosa was available to come for lunch a few days after I had met Jason. I wasn't certain she would come since she left unhappy on her last visit. However, she had called the following day to apologise for being grumpy, so I was hopeful.

There was a lot that we needed to discuss, and I was looking forward to telling her about my baptism, recent experiences and my new understanding. Although God had allowed the massacre of the Jews during World War Two, He was not the one doing it, as I had supposed. I was hoping that I might be able to help Rosa see that God didn't hate or betray her, and kill her family.

I had asked if Terry could come as well, and she had agreed, although somewhat reluctantly.

Terry arrived before Rosa, so we prayed for her visit. This was a new experience, but I was sure our prayer was heard, and this lunch together would be special for Rosa. We asked the Lord to give us the right words so that Rosa would be able to sense our love for her and understand what we wanted to share.

When she arrived, Rosa couldn't take her eyes off Terry. This previously cold-hearted, arrogant lady was now overflowing with warmth, joy and peace.

'What happened to you?' were Rosa's opening words.

We moved to the lounge room and relaxed on my soft old couches, each holding a plate of toasted cheese and tomato sandwiches. I saw some resistance in Rosa when Terry talked about the love of Jesus and how He had transformed her.

I shared my experience of coming to know Jesus, too, and my baptism, but our experiences were causing her some discomfort.

She said, 'I was raised in the church, but I don't have a personal connection with Jesus. You two must be special.'

We asked if she had ever repented and given her life to Jesus when she was in the church. She thought it wasn't necessary as she was raised in the church and had always believed in God.

'I was never a thief, drug dealer or prostitute or did anything bad, but my husband had been a drug dealer, so he had to do those things.'

We did our best to explain, despite being new to the faith, that nobody is good enough to enjoy the life Christ offers.

It is about what Jesus has done for all of us. It is not about how bad our sins are, but that we have all sinned and every one of us needs to repent. When we do, we are forgiven, and that is where this amazing relationship with Jesus begins.

Rosa said she didn't know Jesus but knew about Him. She said her husband, Steve, had that type of personal relationship, but she seemed unable to, so believed she was not worthy.

With a smile, Terry assured her she was right.

'None of us is worthy, Rosa, and that is the amazing part of the story.'

Rosa was a little confused because, for a long time she had been sure a relationship with Jesus was only available for a few special chosen people. Because she assumed she was not one of the special ones, she was jealous of the relationship Steve had with the Lord.

She didn't understand that the key to this relationship is repentance.

I told her that, in the Bible, when all the people at Pentecost asked what they must do to be saved, Peter's answer was not complicated. 'Repent and be baptised,' he said.

'Is it that simple? Can anyone do that? Don't you have to be special or something? I have done neither of those things. I want that relationship you have, but I thought I wasn't special enough. I stopped going to church after Steve died because I was more certain than ever that God hated me. I had tried to find what Steve had, but, as I said, I was convinced I was not chosen. That idea caused me to resent God and think He was unfair.'

She added, 'Do you think it is available for me too?'

We told her He died for us all and longed to welcome her into His family.

With a pained expression, she asked, 'But first, there is something I do not understand. If Jesus is full of love and wants that relationship with us, why did he kill my husband and baby? Why was He punishing me?'

I had been expecting this question.

CHAPTER THIRTY-FIVE

In the days leading up to that moment, I had poured hours into reading, thought and prayer, seeking the answer to that difficult and common question: Why did God allow innocent people to suffer? I also shared the question with Karen and Julia, without mentioning Rosa.

I flipped open my Bible to the Old Testament, and my eyes fell upon the words "The lovingkindness of the Lord is from everlasting to everlasting."

As beautiful as that sounded, I wondered if that was only for some people, so I looked again at some passages Karen had marked. I read about Jesus healing sick people and even raising the dead son of a widow, as he was being carried to his grave. Would the same God kill and also heal? I know we all must die sometime, and Karen had explained that death was the result of sin coming into the world when Adam and Eve disobeyed God. So, if God didn't kill Rosa's husband, then what is the explanation? I had come to an understanding of how to answer this question, not just for Rosa, but for myself also.

'Why do innocent people suffer?' is a question I think we all ask at some point. And they always assume it is God who sends the suffering, forgetting that we live in a fallen world and we have an enemy, Satan, who wants to destroy us and turn us away from God.

With a silent prayer, I shared with Rosa what I had learnt.

'I found some passages in the Bible where Jesus talks about this. The first one is in the book of Luke.

'Jesus commented on the deaths of some people killed in an

accident; "Those eighteen who died when the tower in Siloam fell on them, do you think they were more guilty than all the others living in Jerusalem?" '

I explained, 'Jesus said they were no worse or better than anyone else.'

I told Rosa I found a verse in Matthew saying God allows the sun to shine on the good and the evil and rain to fall on the just and the unjust. That means good and bad things happen to us all. We live in a fallen world, but the good news is that God will help us through those times and use them for our growth.

I said, 'I didn't get angry with God when my husband died as I wasn't convinced God existed anyway, and if He did, I was sure He didn't care.

'I don't think God killed my husband or your husband, Rosa. My husband fell off a ladder that he shouldn't have been on, and your husband died as a result of his plane hitting an unmarked power line. As tragic as both of those deaths are, God didn't kill them.'

Rosa sat still, digesting what she had heard.

"I have never heard this. It does make sense, I guess, as God can't be hateful and loving at the same time.'

Terry and I gasped when she spoke again.

'My pastor had told me I must have done something extremely wicked to deserve this punishment.'

My heart broke, and I grabbed her and hugged her tightly. How could anyone walk through life without a limp, having been told something so cruel?

We talked well into the afternoon, both Terry and I sharing what we knew about God, Jesus and the Holy Spirit.

Rosa came to understand what Jesus was offering her.

She stood and paced the floor for a few silent minutes, and then turned to us and said, 'I want to repent and have the relationship with Jesus that you have.'

Terry and I both cheered.

CHAPTER THIRTY-SIX

'So, how do I do it? I have heard of the 'sinner's prayer'. Do you have a copy that I can read? I must ask Jesus into my heart, right? Is that what I have to do?'

Terry caught my eye and we both smiled. Neither of us had heard of that prayer or about asking Jesus into our hearts. We knew that Peter had said to repent and be baptised, and the Bible says we must believe. Those are the important steps. We explained to Rosa that we need to acknowledge that we are sinners in need of salvation, believe that Jesus came to save us from our sins, paying the ultimate price to save us, by giving His life as a sacrifice for sin, and ask Jesus to forgive us for our sins. We then hand over the reins of our life to Him and make Him our Lord. We were excited but didn't think there were special words she should say or read, as neither of us had done so.

Terry suggested we all get on our knees and told Rosa to tell Jesus whatever she wanted to say.

Rosa began the same way I had.

'Dear Jesus.' And then the floodgates opened.

'I'm so sorry. I'm so sorry. I always blamed You. I yelled at You. I shook my fist at You. I even cursed You. Oh, Jesus, I was so wrong. I understand now that you have loved and cared for me all my life. Oh, please have mercy on me. Please. I don't deserve it. I know that. But please, please forgive me.'

All three of us were on the floor.

After a short while, Terry put her arm around Rosa and said, 'He has, Rosa. The past is forgiven. This is a new day.'

Rosa pulled herself up onto the couch and sat still with her head in her hands. The tears had stopped. We all sat in silence.

Rosa soon lifted her tear-stained face and beamed. Terry and I laughed and clapped.

It was done. As Jesus said, 'Behold I make all things new.'

Laughter and tears followed, and with great excitement, Rosa said, 'OK. Now I need to be baptised. Today. We need a pastor to do it.'

I called Karen to tell her the wonderful news and asked if she or David could come and baptise Rosa, as she wanted to be baptised straight away.

'Why don't you and Terry do it?'

'Oh no. No! We are not qualified.'

Karen chuckled and said, 'Show me in the Bible the qualifications for baptising someone. Who do you suppose baptised John the Baptist? He told Jesus that He should baptise him. Maybe John wasn't even baptised. We don't know. Also, did the one hundred and twenty disciples baptise three thousand people on the Day of Pentecost? I suspect those people baptised each other.'

I had never thought about these practical issues.

Karen added, 'But can I come?'

'Yes, please. Of course. We will meet you at the spot where I was baptised in about half an hour. I will find some old clothes for Rosa. We are about the same size.'

Thirty minutes later, we were standing by the creek. Rosa almost pulled Terry and me into the water. She didn't want to waste a minute. Karen had given us simple instructions on how to do it and what we could say, although our words were not the most important part.

'Our job is to lead people in repentance and put them under the water and bring them up again. That is all. Jesus does the rest,' she said.

We walked out to where the water was waist-deep, and Rosa held her nose while Terry and I lowered her under the water and helped her up again. Rosa's hands flew up in the air, and she started jumping up and down, splashing both of us, laughing loudly.

We came out of the water with hugs and laughter, and then the three of us laid our hands on Rosa and asked the Lord to fill her to overflowing with His Spirit.

Rosa couldn't stop laughing as joy bubbled out of her.

What a wonderful day we had, which none of us will ever forget. There is joy in Heaven, and on Earth also, when someone comes to Jesus in repentance.

After Rosa had showered and dressed at my place, she said she was going straight to see Charlotte to tell her all about it.

Filled with peace and joy at that moment, I had no warning of the devastating blow to hit us the very next day.

CHAPTER THIRTY-SEVEN

Tuesday was book club again. I arrived early, as I had offered to help Karen get set up for our meeting. I found her sitting on her front steps, crying. I was confused, so I sat with her until she could speak.

'It's Rosa,' Karen sobbed, 'Oh Rosa.' I put my arm over her shoulder and waited, as she buried her head in her hands.

'Rosa is in the hospital.'

Trying to breathe between sobs, Karen added, 'Last night she was in a terrible car accident.'

'What??' I must have misunderstood.

'Rosa? But we were with her yesterday.'

Tearfully, Karen said, 'On her way home from Charlotte's last night, Rosa may have been going a bit fast or not concentrating on her driving after the day's excitement. Sometime around ten o'clock last night, a car came upon her car on its side against a tree. There was a huge dead Eastern Grey nearby. Rosa was the one who had always warned us to watch out for kangaroos on the road at night.'

She buried her face in her hands again and continued to cry as I sat beside her, stunned. She told me she and Charlotte had spent the night at the hospital by her side, while through the night, the doctors had been fighting to save her life.

Karen had known Rosa for over six years, and they had become firm friends, although Karen had not been able to persuade her to come to church. Rosa had never shared with Karen the reason she didn't want to go.

'If you want to go back to the hospital, I will set up the chairs and tea things and take care of the book club. I will share about Rosa's car accident and that you are with her.'

She nodded and hurried towards her car. With Karen, Charlotte and Rosa absent, we were a smaller group than usual. I told everyone about Rosa's accident but had few details. A couple said they would try and visit her later that day or perhaps the following day. I didn't say anything. I was sure she was seriously hurt, but didn't want to alarm anyone until we had more information. I could see that Brenda knew I was worried.

I added my comments about the latest book, about a man who thought he could predict the future. The conversation was lively, with varied opinions and the usual enthusiasm, but I couldn't get excited about it. There was no way I could have predicted Rosa's accident the previous night, so I found the book irritating. My mind was at the hospital, although I tried to look as though I was engaged in the discussion.

I was the last to leave after we had washed Karen's cups and saucers. As I closed the front door, Karen's husband, David, whom I had met before, drove in. As I greeted him when he climbed the steps on their porch, his face bore the unmistakable signs of grief. He looked deep into my eyes, held my hands and sighed.

'Rosa didn't make it, Louisa.'

I sank onto the steps, feeling the full force of the blow. I foolishly assumed she was going to be fine but was immediately thankful that Jesus had saved her soul. My thoughts went straight to poor Charlotte and her family.

I have learnt in the short time I have been born again, that God is merciful, just and righteous. The death of family and friends is inevitable in this life and something we all face and must bear, even though it is extremely painful.

David said, 'Karen was able to talk to Rosa for a short while before she slipped into a coma, and had assured her that Jesus was waiting to receive her into His glorious presence. Rosa had smiled and then closed her eyes for the last time.'

The funeral was scheduled for the following Wednesday. In the meantime, we had the painful task of telling friends the sad news.

I called Julia first, dreading being the bearer of such shocking news. She had just arrived home from the book club and was shocked and saddened. We had both been sure she would recover and get to live a long life as a new child of God. No one knows how long they will live, which gives a greater urgency to tell people about Jesus as soon as possible. I hated to think where Rosa would be now if we hadn't led her to Jesus the day before. We prayed together for Charlotte, and Julia said she would go and tell Terry, and they would pray too.

I called Irene and told her, and she was shocked. She said she would let Marianne and Joanna know. I said I would drop by the cafe and tell Brenda, but I was grateful not to have to be the bearer of such shocking news to everyone.

When I walked into the cafe, Brenda gave me a big smile, until she saw my face. I think she then knew what I was going to tell her. She ushered me into her office and closed the door.

Her shoulders sagged as she took my hand and said, 'She has gone, hasn't she….'

I nodded. Brenda collapsed into her chair and stared straight ahead, letting out a long, slow sigh.I then realised that Brenda didn't know what happened the day before, so I filled her in on Rosa's salvation and baptism. She was amazed and relieved.

'As sad as I am that she has left us, my sadness is mixed with joy, knowing that she is with Jesus. Nothing matters compared to knowing Jesus. Today you have brought both sad and wonderful news.'

Both of our hearts went out to Charlotte and her children, and we spent several minutes there in Brenda's office praying for them.

We prayed that the news Rosa had shared the night before

would have a positive impact on Charlotte, despite the pain. We were sure it was now far from her mind, as she would be focusing on trying to come to terms with the reality of her sister's death. The children would be devastated to lose their dear aunty, but I doubted that the younger ones would grasp the impact of her death immediately. Jason and Anna would feel it and understand the pain their mother was going through.

I expected Jason would want to cancel milking on Saturday, so I sent him a message. He asked if he could please still come. He may have needed to be with someone outside the family and get away from the grief-filled home for a short while.

CHAPTER THIRTY-EIGHT

Saturday at 6:30 sharp, Jason arrived on his bike. I hugged him without thinking, and he started to cry. He was embarrassed as he hadn't shed any tears after hearing about his aunt. I held him for several minutes as he sobbed quietly. He eventually stepped back, saying that he wanted to be strong for his mum. I encouraged him to cry as it was healthy and normal. He then sat on my couch and cried and sniffed for some minutes. I handed him a fistful of tissues and sat with my arm around his shoulders. When he recovered, he looked at me with a slight smile and gave me a quick kiss on my cheek.

Then he leapt to his feet, saying, 'Let's go and milk Bessie.' He was ready for a distraction.

My beautiful cow Bessie has a pale tan coat, like a creamy cup of milk coffee. Her big, deep brown eyes are a signature trait of all pure Jersey cows. Her gentle temperament is a distinct advantage, as she even allows my grandchildren to sit on her back as she chews her cud. She also remains still with a novice milker, if she has her breakfast while we milk her. This is the routine I began when I inherited her, and I have adhered to it ever since.

I can't describe the soothing effect of the rhythmical sound of the milk squirting into the bucket, the contented sound of a cow methodically eating her way through her breakfast, and the pleasure of leaning against her warm body while milking. I always have a chat with Bessie to start my day, my morning routine, no matter the weather.

I showed Jason how to lead Bessie into her stall and tie her up with the old frayed rope I had been using since I arrived. He helped me get some feed to keep her still while we milked. I pulled over the traditional three-legged milking stool, and I sat down to give Jason his first milking lesson as he watched over my shoulder.

I taught him how to place his fingers on the teats and apply light pressure, starting with his pointer finger and working rhythmically down the teat, one finger at a time, forcing the milk out. He was eager to try, so we swapped places.

I could sense his excitement as he settled onto the stool and reached for the teats. It warmed my heart to see his enthusiasm. I love to rest my head against her flank and feel the warmth of her body, so I smiled as I saw Jason do the same. His hands were bigger than mine, but his fingers were nimble. He took to milking naturally and was delighted with his results. He was talking to Bessie as he milked her, which was sweet. He was starting to love her the same way that I did.

He took the milk to my separator, poured it in and cranked the handle.

'Wow, look at all that cream, Grandma! I didn't know there was so much cream in milk. Can I put heaps of this on my pancakes?'

We carried the milk and cream into the kitchen after we had returned Bessie to her paddock.

I then set out the ingredients for the pancakes and discovered that Jason was already an expert. He told me they were a Sunday tradition at his house, but never with fresh cream.

With a stack of blueberry pancakes, fresh cream and golden syrup, we settled down to enjoy the fruit of our labour.

After pancakes with several spoonsful of cream, Jason started to talk about his aunt.

'Aunty Rosa used to do many things for us. Now I feel like I didn't ever thank her enough. She even used to take us on holidays with her. As a kid, I never understood the cost of those trips or how generous she was. She would always come and see us as soon as she got home from one of her business trips and would bring treats for us kids or a meal, to give Mum a break.' Tears fell as he talked about how hard it was going to be for his mum without the help of her sister.

'Aunty Rosa was seven years older than Mum, and Mum was always proud of her. She looked up to her as her example. Their mother died when Mum was little, so Aunty Rosa was sort of like her mother. I know Mum is going to be lonely. Aunty Rosa was all the family she had.'

I didn't know how to comfort him, but I was determined to do whatever I could to help Charlotte and her grieving children.

When Jason was about to leave, he turned to me, hugged me, and thanked me for teaching him how to milk Bessie and for the milk and cream he was taking home. He remarked that he had a good morning.

But his parting statement disturbed me. He asked me to sit with him at his aunt's funeral on Wednesday, but I wanted to tell him I had no intention of going. I planned to send my sympathies with beautiful flowers and make a casserole for his family, but I didn't plan to step inside that church. So, I had a problem. I had to go.

CHAPTER THIRTY-NINE

Wednesday came too fast and the dread had been rising daily. I loved Rosa, but to go into the church was going to be too difficult. I thought about calling Jason and telling him I would meet him at the graveside, but I knew that was wrong, and it could jeopardise my fledgling relationship with him. I felt honoured that he had asked me to sit with him. It showed me that our relationship was as important to him as it was to me.

I called Karen on Monday and explained my predicament. I had told her before that I would not go to her church, and she had not pressured me. She assured me I had nothing to fear and I could sit with Jason and relax, but I wasn't sure it would be that easy. I had never been inside a church building, except for a few weddings. I had seen services occasionally in movies, and I didn't like the nonsense I saw. Robes, statues, parades, candles and dreary music. I prayed all weekend that the Lord would give me the strength to go into that place.

I had no idea what they did during funerals in churches, but I hoped her body would not be there in the box up front with the lid open. I could never concentrate at a funeral when they did that.

The funeral was at 10:00 a.m., and Julia and I arrived together. I felt braver having her with me, and she prayed with me beforehand.

I walked in and saw immediately that the church was nothing like I had seen in movies. The interior of the building was not what I had imagined, as there were no candles or statues as I had expected. It was not sombre, melancholy or religious, as a quiet hum of chatter filled the building, where I saw many familiar faces. There was no dirge-like music playing softly to make us all feel more miserable.

I found Jason with his family in the front row, with the empty seat he had saved for me. His face lit up when he saw me, and as I sat beside him, I gave his arm a little squeeze and smiled at Charlotte, who was doing her best to hold herself together. She gave me a slight nod and then looked straight ahead again, staring intently at nothing. Such a difficult day for Charlotte, who was doing her best to get through it.

Karen's husband moved to the front of the church. Without a robe, sour face, candles or smelly stuff, David smiled and welcomed Rosa's friends and family.

The service started with the singing of 'Amazing Grace' and 'Thine be the Glory', which I later learnt are two well-known hymns. The words were powerful and seemed to lift the atmosphere in the church as they were both sung enthusiastically. I thought this couldn't be what church here was usually like.

I knew there were some of Rosa's work colleagues present, so I was praying for them to be touched by the service.

David read the eulogy, which had been prepared by Charlotte and her family. Rosa and Charlotte had no siblings, which would make Charlotte feel alone, like being lost in a vast crowd searching for a familiar face.

As David talked about Rosa, as often happens at funerals, we learnt a lot about her life. She graduated from university at a young age and was recognised as a research pioneer in computer science, and was credited with significant advances in her field, which had an important impact on our military. Most people did not know that she had been in the Air Force. She had never boasted about her accomplishments, although I knew Charlotte had been proud of her.

Since I had the opportunity to become acquainted with

Rosa, I had been looking forward to our times together, even more so after she was born again. I added to the sniffles and sobs around me.

Finishing the eulogy, David looked at the people and said, 'Rosa came to know Jesus on the day of her death. Asking Jesus to forgive her for her sins and yielding her life to Him was the most important decision she ever made, and I know that she is now in the arms of Jesus. Our acknowledgement of our sins and Jesus' sacrifice for us determines where we will spend eternity.

'We all must recognise our need for a saviour,' he said, 'and call out to Jesus, as Rosa did. The Bible says we have all sinned, and Jesus has paid the price for us to be reconciled to God. Nothing compares to the joy we experience when we know we are forgiven.'

I suspected that people were examining their own relationship with God. Funerals have a way of confronting people with their mortality, and David took the opportunity to remind us that we do not know when our lives will end.

He told the parable from Luke 18 about two men going to the temple to pray. One said to himself that he was thankful that he wasn't like other men but was a good man who paid his tithes and fasted twice a week. He compared himself to others who were not living a life as upright as his and didn't see himself in need of forgiveness.

In contrast, the other man recognised he was a sinner and was asking God for mercy. Jesus had asked the crowd which one went home forgiven. The answer was obviously the one who humbled himself before God and knew he needed forgiveness. David asked the people if they thought they could win God's approval through their good deeds and be accepted into God's kingdom.

David shared how some people think that God will accept them into heaven when they die, as they have been good, and perhaps have attended church regularly. They may think, like the man in the parable, that they will go to heaven, but they have never humbled themselves and realised their need for a saviour and repented and asked for forgiveness. The most horrifying words anyone could ever hear would be God saying, 'Sorry, I never knew you. Depart from me.' David said these words may be heard by some regular churchgoers who have never repented and entered into a saving relationship with Jesus.

Rosa's sudden and unexpected death was a sober warning that no one should wait and plan to come to Jesus at a later time.

This was the first funeral I had attended where the preacher offered people hope of eternal life. For me, funerals had always been miserable, negative experiences at a dreary funeral parlour. I had never heard a message like this, and I enjoyed listening to it, knowing I had made peace with God.

From where I was sitting, I noticed people with their eyes fixed on the floor as David was talking. I was praying for the people who had not yet acknowledged their need for a saviour. The church was crowd-ed, with some unfamiliar faces. I suspected some people who loved Rosa had come a long way to be part of the service. Her sudden death was naturally a shock.

Unfortunately, not everyone was pleased with David's message.

An elegant, bejewelled lady loudly remarked as she left the church that the message and the Bible story were both highly inappropriate for a funeral service. With her nose in the air, looking as if she had just smelt something unpleasant, she added, 'I don't know who this pastor is, but he is clearly not a loving man. I won't be coming here again.'

I didn't know a more loving man, and I couldn't think of a better message to preach.

I did notice that only some of her friends muttered their agreement, but not all of them. I was sure some were affected by David's words and considering their own relationship with God. Many people think sitting in a church building every Sunday and perhaps reading the verse of the day gives them a 'ticket' to heaven. They have no idea about growing in knowledge and understanding of God, laying down their will and making Jesus Lord of their lives. It is about relationship, not duties.

I joined the crowd in the churchyard. It could have been a graveside scene from a movie, with cold drizzle, thick dark clouds and dripping black umbrellas bobbing silently towards the grave.

There was a quiet crowd around the grave with all eyes on the casket about to be lowered into the ground. David talked for a short while about the final resurrection of the dead on the day that Jesus returns, saying that those who know Him will rise to meet Him in the air on His return. He then turned his eyes to Charlotte and the children and prayed a compassionate and sincere prayer of comfort.

Chairs were set up for the immediate family, but Charlotte and her family had chosen to stand. The children were all clinging to Charlotte, crying quietly, trying to comfort their mother as well as draw comfort from her. The sounds of sobbing could be heard throughout the crowd, with perhaps more tears for the heartbroken family than for the one who was now with her Saviour.

Charlotte and her children each threw a rose onto the coffin as it was being lowered into the ground. It was heart-wrenching to watch. As everyone walked quietly from the graveside, heading into the church hall for refreshments, I turned to see Charlotte and her children standing alone, huddled together beside the grave. That scene cut even more deeply into my heart than their tears. I wanted to go and comfort them all, but I had no words that would make the day any easier for them.

After the burial, I joined everyone in the church hall and I was pleased to catch up with several of the townspeople, despite the occasion. All of the book club ladies were there with their families, offering love and support to Charlotte and her children. Jason found me and stayed by my side for quite some time, and I took hold of his hand and smiled weakly at his tear-stained face. After a while, he went to stand with his mother, doing all he could to give her the support she needed.

Feeling relaxed but sad, I was shocked by a sudden, painful stab in my chest. Looking around the room while munching on a lamington and drinking a mug of hot tea, I saw him.

CHAPTER FORTY

I knew without a doubt it was him. The face from years ago was still vivid in my memory. He had aged, of course, but greying hair and a few wrinkles did not disguise him. I dropped the lamington and, with a trembling hand, after spilling tea on my blouse, placed the mug on a nearby table. Gasping for air, I rushed out of the building. I headed for the nearby bushes where I threw up the lamington, the tea and my breakfast.

That is where Julia found me.

'Julia, Julia, help me!! He's here, he is here!'

I clutched her arms and couldn't let go. I was breathing hard, crying and shaking.

'Don't let him see me. Don't let him come near me. Please, I have to get away. I have to go.'

I don't remember how she got me home, but I vowed I would never go near that church again.

While Julia drove, she tried to get me to calm down and think more rationally, helping me to realise that I was in no danger from him, and having seen him once, I would be okay the next time I saw him. The problem with this first sighting was that it was unexpected. When she dropped me home, I lied, assuring her I was fine. I walked inside, locked the door, lay on my couch and stared at the ceiling for a few hours, trying to cope.

Dorjan Halmi. What was he doing at the funeral? Did he attend the church? I knew the answer to the second question. He wouldn't want to go there, and since Karen knew about his past, she and David wouldn't allow him to set foot inside anyway. People like him are not welcome in churches, I was sure. The nuns had told me things like that.

I guess he had known Rosa from the supermarket, but I still thought he had a nerve stepping inside a church, even for a funeral. When I saw him, he was chatting to some people I didn't know, acting like he was a normal person. I guess they didn't know that there was nothing normal about him. He was an animal, not a human. He belonged in a cage.

I was shocked at how quickly my thoughts were spiralling downward—growing more irrational and more unkind the longer I lay there. I had to get up and get busy, as I knew these ungodly thoughts were hurting me and not him.

I realised I needed to turn these negative, unfair thoughts into something positive, so I asked the Lord to bless Dorjan Halmi in his new life in Wattle Creek. I didn't think that would mean I should ever talk to him, but it quieted the ugly storm within, and restored my peace.

Having repented from my self-centred life, I planned to reach out to my friends as I was determined to focus on their needs instead of my own. I naively thought this was the solution to the problem of Dorjan Halmi's presence in Wattle Creek.

CHAPTER FORTY-ONE

I found myself eagerly anticipating Jason's visits, feeling a spark of joy whenever I saw his bike heading my way. He sometimes dropped by for a quick visit on his way home from school, and I always had a snack ready for him. Some days he talked about his aunt, and sometimes he asked questions about my life in Hungary.

He would usually stay about half an hour before he headed home to do his homework. Charlotte knew this was often his routine and was happy for him to drop by.

She told me, 'I would rather he visit you than be out in the street with the friends he used to spend his time with. I know he is seeing them less these days, and I'm glad about that.'

After milking one Saturday morning, when Jason and I were sitting relaxing on my back verandah, eating porridge with golden syrup and plenty of cream, he asked me about the ghetto in Hungary.

'We heard a bit about the war in history class, but it didn't sound real to me, like something ages ago and far away. It only became real when I read what you had written and sent home with Mum. Mum had left your letter lying around, but I didn't read all of it. Can you tell me what the ghetto was like for you, Grandma?'

I didn't want to tell him the worst of it, but I hoped I could give him a general idea.

'Well, Jason, it is impossible to paint a pretty picture of what it was like. We Jews were not the only ones sent there. The Nazis also arrested homosexuals, gypsies, the disabled and all who didn't support Hitler, even the most intelligent and learned. People were killed or beaten, women were abused, and everyone was scared. It is one thing to get a fright and then feel okay, but it is exhausting to be frightened night and day without any relief. People died in the ghettos throughout Europe, Jason, of cold, disease, or starvation.

'They were stinking dirty places with poor sanitation, always in the worst parts of towns.

'The ghetto in Budapest, set up by the Arrow Cross regime in November, covered just a quarter of a square kilometre, but housed seventy thousand people. Jason, that is about the size of two Australian football fields. Can you imagine that many people in a space that small? The Germans forced us to live under miserable conditions. Such a nightmare for all of us, as we were treated like animals, even by fellow Hungarians.'

I told Jason how Jews had all contact with the outside world taken away and were not allowed to leave the ghettos, so they were treated like prisoners.

The creation of ghettos was a key step in the Nazi process of brutally separating, persecuting, and working towards eliminating all of Europe's Jews.

'We were fortunate in Budapest, as we were there for just a few months, although it felt like years. Mum and I shared a room with strangers. There were nine of us in one room, and we were all hungry and scared.'

Jason was surprised. 'Nine people in one room? That sounds crazy. Nine in one house is a lot, but all sharing one room? Where did you sleep? Were there nine beds?

'No, Jason, we didn't have any beds. We mainly sat on the floor and tried to sleep leaning against the wall.'

'Where did you get your food?'

'We used some of our items to barter for food. We were taken so unexpectedly that all we could do was grab some essentials. Fortunately, my mother had grabbed a blanket, which was helpful to combat the cold. We were given meagre rations, which we knew would not sustain us, and indeed were not designed to.

'My mother sent me out at night to see what I could find to eat. I was your age, Jason, and through hunger and desperation, I resorted, I'm ashamed to say, to stealing.'

'But Grandma, you were hungry.'

'I was desperate to get enough food for my mother as she was getting thinner and frailer every day. The others in our room had their problems getting enough food, and I am afraid it was 'every man for himself'. My main concern was to look after my mother.

'There were some sympathetic non-Jewish Hungarians who smuggled food for us, often during the night, although the guards did their best to prevent outsiders from helping us. We all were living a nightmare, but compared to other European countries, and our Jewish brothers and sisters outside of Budapest, our trial was short-lived. We were treated cruelly, even though we were innocent of any crime except being born a Jew.

'People were being transported out of the ghetto by the hundreds to concentration camps or labour camps. We did not know anything about these at the time, but the way the people were being treated like cattle, we knew it was a bad sign.'

'After the war, we found out that the ghettos in some Hungarian cities were worse than what we experienced. In some places, Jews were forced to live outdoors, without shelter or sanitary facilities, in the bitter cold. Food and water supplies were low, and medical care was non-existent. Did you read the part in your mum's letter about how we were rescued from there?'

(Charlotte had assured me that Jason had not read about Dorjan. She told me she threw away those pages after she read it, just in case her children saw it. I was very grateful.)

'Oh yes. That was amazing, Grandma. I cried when I read that part.'

I had shared enough about the ghetto, as I didn't want Jason to think it was exciting like he saw in movies. I tried to explain that the constant fear and panic were like being lost in a dark maze, with no hope of finding a way out.

Jason was satisfied with what I told him that morning and went to collect the eggs for me and left soon after to go home and help his mother.

'I spent the afternoon reading our book for book club as the day was approaching, and I hadn't opened the new one yet.

I didn't enjoy the book as it was sad and based on a true story. The book was dark, and I was not surprised when I heard that others were not enjoying it either.

I expected Tuesday's meeting to be an interesting one, but this book upset one lady in particular.

CHAPTER FORTY-TWO

This book was badly timed, considering what we had been through with the death of Rosa. The librarian, Margaret, chose our books well in advance, and we hoped to have a happy one. Unfortunately, this was not the case. It was called *Who Took My Little Girl?* about a missing child. It was based on a true story from the late nineteenth century of a girl who had been snatched from her mother in a crowded street and was never seen again, despite a country-wide search and news coverage. About twenty years later, some hikers had found her remains in a shallow grave in bushland west of Sydney in the Blue Mountains.

I noticed Joanna looked uncomfortable and was not contributing to the discussion. Joanna, who is a retired graphic designer, came from France as a child and is a carer for her aged mother. She is quietly spoken and is not a big contributor to the book discussions, but she always reads the books and never misses a meeting. The few comments she makes are always insightful as she is a deep thinker but of few words. Her eyes filled with tears, and she ran from the room and sat on Karen's verandah. None of us knew what to do or say. Karen suggested that we leave her alone for a while, which turned out to be the right advice. We tried to carry on with our discussion, but our attention was on the verandah. After a while, Joanna bravely re-entered the room, apologised unnecessarily and was silent for the rest of our meeting. This book had unearthed some pain from Joanna's past, but no one forced her to talk. I was familiar with how past pain could unexpectedly resurface, so I was determined to pray for her.

I heard a quiet tap on my door the following afternoon and Joanna smiled weakly as I ushered her in with a hug. We sat on my back verandah with our mugs of coffee, and I waited for her to talk.

She opened by saying something similar to what I had heard from Irene. Since I had shared my pain, she dared to share hers.

'I had a sister four years younger than me, Louisa. One cold winter's night, my parents, my sister Celina, and I went walking in the middle of Paris, enjoying the beautiful Christmas lights. We were amongst the crowds of sightseers marvelling at the beauty and the atmosphere, until my mother stopped abruptly. "Where is Celina?"

'A wave of terror crashed over us as we frantically searched the crowd, calling her name. A police officer helped us search and radioed other officers in the area. My parents gave a detailed description of her appearance and her clothes, but we found no trace of her. The newspapers over the following several days carried a picture of her, with the shocking headline, 'MISSING'.'

She said, 'Like you with your brother, we never found out what happened to her, if she was hurt, abused and scared, killed or even taken to another country. You understand the torture of not knowing.'

She started to cry. Not softly, but deep soul-wracking sobs, as if years of grief were finally released from their dark and lonely prison. I held her as she moistened my shoulder. Suppressed pain was being released, no longer under her control. Finally, her shoulders sagged and she pulled away.

'I'm sorry, Louisa. I didn't mean to cry. I have never cried like that.'

As I wiped my eyes, I assured her there was no need to apologise—I understood the pain of loss, the ache of uncertainty, and the torture of all the "if onlys."

'I should have been holding her hand, and I should have been watching her closely.'

She started, and I had to stop her.

'No, Joanna. Don't go there. You are heading down a path that has twists and turns and has no end.'

She nodded slowly, understanding where she was heading. Like me, she had been down that torturous road too often.

'My mother became depressed, and both my parents seemed to forget they still had one daughter. Our home was filled with gloom, and there was never the sound of laughter again. I tried to stay out of my parents' way, and Celina's name was not allowed to be mentioned. I was only ten and had no way to process my grief, as I had no one to talk to. It sounds silly, but every night I would line up my dolls in the dark and tell them the whole story over and over. I was compliant and quiet so as not to upset my parents. But I was a lonely, hurting child, often frightened that one day I might disappear like Celina. I was too scared to go out to play with my friends, and no one understood why. I spent most of my time in my bedroom, feeling safer there and out of my parents' way. It was in those days, months and years that I was an avid reader, devouring books to escape into imaginary worlds. It was my love of books that excited me about the new book club.'

She was silent for a while, staring into her past, and then added, 'I have carried this grief with me all my life, Louisa, as I have searched for a way to be free of it.'

Taking my hand and looking deep into my eyes, she added, 'I came today because I knew you would understand, but also, I want to know how you cope with the pain. I read your story, and it was far worse than what I have had to deal with. You locked yourself away, which I fully understand, but since then, you have been different. I don't see that pain in you, so I want to know your coping mechanism. Is it meditation, yoga, exercise, or have you become a Buddhist or something? Another religion? I have visited three psychologists without my mother knowing. They have recognised the symptoms of childhood trauma, but were not able to give me a solution. They have all told me that I have the classic signs, as I am insecure, have low self-esteem, suffer from needless anxiety and don't cope well with change. These are symptoms of a problem that they have repeatedly told me has no cure. I had to learn to recognise these symptoms, acknowledge their cause and learn to cope with them. However, watching you, I have seen a change that has given me hope that there must be some key to healing that I have not heard of before.'

I wanted her to understand that I still had some issues to deal with, mainly the problem of that one man, so I tried to explain what I was experiencing.

'Joanna, I am no better than you and no stronger than you. After suffering for years, I knew that there was nothing in me that could overcome the pain, and like you, I was feeling hopeless and helpless.

'Things came to a climax when I heard Dorjan was in town. I had suppressed my pain and kept busy, believing that ignoring it would cause it to disappear, and I would eventually feel whole again. You and I both know, it doesn't work. For me, the trigger that reopened the wounds was Dorjan's arriving; for you, it has been this latest novel. There is always something that will tear the wounds open when we think we have healed and we have moved forward.

Joanna, with eyes wide, nodded vigorously. 'So, please tell me, what has made the difference for you?'

In the next hour, I told Joanna how I learnt about Jesus and that He is our Messiah. I shared my struggles and how God has guided me in my search for truth and healing.For the following meeting, Joanna made possibly the most difficult treat from *Bickering Bakers*, which was a delicious work of art.

I hoped that she was trying to process what I had shared with her about Jesus. Brenda had suggested we make something difficult from the book if we were ever feeling stressed. Joanna looked uncomfortable after our talk, so I thought this may have been the reason for her gourmet masterpiece. Maybe it was a sign that she was feeling challenged.

CHAPTER FORTY-THREE

The following day, I drove to meet Irene for a game of tennis. I was looking forward to it as I was trying to deal with the loss of my friend, Rosa, and keeping busy and focusing on others and their needs was helping me to cope. Irene's ankle had healed enough for a short game, provided she kept it strapped.

We played a few poor games, and I invited Irene to join me for lunch at Common Ground. We talked for a while with Brenda about Rosa and poor Charlotte, and mentioned Joanna and the pain that she is carrying. We were determined to do all we could to support Charlotte and her family and be available to Joanna as well.

Soon, Brenda needed to hurry away and deal with the lunchtime crowd.

Irene, of course, had been at the funeral, and she mentioned that she didn't see me leave as she had hoped to have a chat. I was pleased that she hadn't noticed my hasty exit, as I didn't want to talk about that with anyone. I changed the subject and told Irene about Jason and his milking lesson. She was pleased to hear he was spending time with me, as she had heard from Charlotte that he was interested in farming.

I drew a breath and asked her about Malcolm.

'How are things at home?'

She did look more relaxed than recently, so I took that as a positive sign.

She said,' After you 'forced' me to tell Karen, Malcolm and

David have spent some time together. Karen organised for David to visit Malcolm, and as they both are golfers, they have played some games together.'

She told me that after a short time, Malcolm opened up to David about his loss of identity since leaving his successful profession. He even confessed he had been unkind to Irene. This provided an opening for David, and he was able to help Malcolm cope with these feelings. David felt it was important to have someone who understands and will listen. Irene has seen changes in Malcolm, and he has even apologised for how he had been treating her. I was very pleased to hear about definite progress in such a short time. Irene added that he wasn't perfect, and still sometimes was short-tempered, but he could see where he was heading and regain control of his emotions.

Irene then said, 'Louisa, I know you have been well acquainted with pain in your life. I feel that what I have been through with Malcolm is trivial compared with what you and your family, and indeed all the Jews in Europe, have suffered. I am not religious, but I could never turn on people of any faith. If people want to believe in supernatural things, they should be free in any country to do so. I don't of course, as I think there was some 'Big Bang' somewhere in space and so we are born, we live, and when we die, it's all over.'

I asked her, "Haven't you ever looked closely at a flower and marvelled at its beauty? Or watched a bird in flight, or held a newborn baby, and thought surely this couldn't exist without a Creator?"

Irene looked uncomfortable and changed the subject, asking me to tell her what it was like for my mother and me to be placed in an unfamiliar culture.

I was disappointed with the change, but I love her, so will pray for her and leave her in the Lord's hands.

'Sure, Irene. Let's grab some dessert.'

CHAPTER FORTY-FOUR

While eating our vanilla slices, Irene started, 'As you know, Louisa, I have always lived in Wattle Creek. I cannot imagine arriving in Australia as a foreigner. I heard there were hostels set up for war refugees, so was that where you and your mother were placed?'

'Yes, it is. We were among all those new arrivals. We arrived by plane at Sydney Airport, although hundreds came by boat, and we were taken by train about two hundred kilometres from Sydney to Kelso station and then by bus to a migrant hostel in Kelso which is near Bathurst, the oldest town outside of Sydney.

'The conditions were better than in any ghetto in Europe, but the accommodation was not comfortable. We were staying in army huts which were made of tin and not insulated, making them very hot in summer and cold in winter. There was no privacy, and the camp was overcrowded. When it was erected for army use, it was made to house fifteen hundred soldiers, but after the war, tents had to be erected to house up to eight thousand people at one time.

'Despite the difficulties, optimism was still high among all of the migrants who had come from devastated Europe looking for a fresh start. Various languages were spoken there, and my mother was able to communicate with a number of migrants in their native language, and gain some lifelong friends.

'Most were skilled workers, their main disadvantages being their lack of English or their qualifications not being recognised in Australia.

'I'll tell you something no one expected. When we entered the camp, there was a boom gate that closed behind us. Some of our fellow passengers on the bus panicked as we entered, as the boom gate was too similar to the entrance of the concentration camps. Their fear was overwhelming, and for Mum and I to see their reaction made us even more thankful that we had not experienced the horrors of a concentration camp. I don't know if those people ever recovered from the nightmare they had lived through. The look on their faces was sheer terror, just from the sight of a similar boom gate.'

Irene was shocked. 'That is heart-breaking. All innocent people! But how did you all cope with the cultural changes, Louisa? I heard that you were expected to abandon your native languages and culture and assimilate as quickly as possible into the Australian way of life. That must have been difficult. At least you and your mother had learnt some English before you came here, right?'

'We coped quite well with the cultural changes, having had England as a stepping stone on our journey here. Our English was better than most of the immigrants, so we were given more responsible work.

The Department of Immigration did a good job looking after us all, and we stayed in the camp for only four weeks. We were then both given jobs in Bathurst, and Mum and I both worked as domestics for two years. It was a humbling experience for my mother, who was used to employing such people, but she worked cheerfully, happy to feel safe again. It was clear evidence that my mother was truly transformed.

'Bathurst is where I went to teachers' college when it first opened in 1951, and it was there that I met my late husband, Andrew and Julia.'

I told Irene that the relaxed disposition of Australians was foreign to us, as we were used to rigidity and formality.

'You Australians are informal in your manner and speech,

even to strangers. My mother and I were shocked when we were called 'Love ' or 'Honey' by strangers.'

Irene laughed and was surprised as she had never thought about Australians sounding rude to foreigners.

I smiled and said, 'We found it disconcerting but we soon realised that Australians, in general, were kind to immigrants, 'New Australians' as we were called. Some Australians called us 'reffos', short for refugees, but they didn't say it in a mean way. A lot of migrants did not like the 'New Australian' label, but it made my mother and me feel welcome and gave us a sense of belonging.

'Over time, we became increasingly comfortable referring to ourselves as Australians.'

We talked well into the afternoon, and I headed home at about three, in time for my grocery delivery. Julia and Terry both came for dinner to share the lamb chops, asparagus and ice cream that I hadn't ordered.

While we ate, we spent time talking about the town's upcoming Spring Fair, wondering if there was a way the book club could be involved.

Julia was heading up the committee again this year, as I had heard she had done an excellent job several years in a row. No one wanted her to quit, but each year she told me, 'This is the last year I am doing it.' But then the following year, she would be back in the saddle again.

CHAPTER FORTY-FIVE

The Spring Fair is an annual tradition in our town. It is held in October when we are hopeful that the winter frosts have finished, and the hot summer weather has not yet begun. In Australia, the weather is not predictable, so despite good planning, Spring Fairs have had deep frosts in the past, or blistering dry heat has arrived several weeks too early. This year, the long-range forecast predicted a warm and sunny day.

Since Julia was the chair of the committee, we learned from her that some book club members would be tied up with other clubs and activities—either their own or their children's. We decided we needed to contribute something that would not require a lot of us participating on the day, as most were helping on school or sports club stalls.

We had a special meeting at Julia's on a Thursday to discuss how we might participate in the fair to make our club's existence visible to the community. Irene and I cancelled our regular Thursday tennis game to join in. We were considering a stall until someone suggested we could perhaps put a float in the parade. Julia was excited, saying there were only a few floats entered this year. The town's new fire truck and bulldozer would be in the parade, and our mayor was expected to be riding in an open vintage car, made available each year by the Vintage Car Club. Most of their cars would be in the parade, as usual, or on display near the park. The school planned to have a float with children singing Australian traditional songs, and Julia was hoping a few of the clubs might enter floats too. The church was organising a used book stall and offering prayer, and the football club was having their traditional cake stall, which was always a huge success. The quilting group, which some of our members had joined, would have quilting demonstrations and sell fabric. There would also be the high school's famous 'sausage sizzle' stall. After much discussion and a few cups of tea, we decided to decorate a float. This was a popular idea, as it was a project we could do together before the fair, and only a few of us would be needed to man the float on the day. This was a huge undertaking, which made us all both nervous and excited.

First, we needed a truck or utility, which the locals call a ute. The man who owned the farm behind my place, Jack Thomas, had the perfect-sized one. No one could think of another that could be spared from farm duties to be decorated, and therefore out of commission, for at least the week before the fair. We all knew Mr Thomas, and I was elected to go and ask him if he could lend us his truck. It was rarely out of his shed, so we knew it wasn't being used often. We would promise to clean it and return it full of petrol, which sounded like a fair deal.

'Speak of the devil,' I exclaimed, turning to Julia, 'Isn't that one of Mr Thomas's cows in your paddock?'

Julia agreed, so she and Charlotte went to 'shoo' her home as the rest of us left.

I was a bit nervous about visiting Mr Thomas, so I asked Marianne to join me. I hadn't spoken to him for several months, and he had a reputation for being reclusive, especially since his wife died.

Marianne had given a brief outline of her life at our first book club meeting. Her husband, Alan, is in a wheelchair due to an accident at work several years ago. They have had a very tough few years as their only son died about three years ago. We did not know their son, as Marianne and Alan moved to Wattle Creek about six months after the accident happened. I didn't know Marianne well, so I thought this would be something we could do together, and I could get to know her better.

Marianne was available the following morning while Alan was having his physiotherapy, so we planned on visiting Mr

Thomas and having lunch together afterwards.

We drove in Marianne's car to his farmhouse the following day. I hadn't seen it up close for quite some time, and it looked run down and overgrown. His orchard had grass and weeds that were threatening to hide his unpruned fruit trees. I was surprised as his farm was usually tidy even from a distance, with fences mended, fruit trees pruned, and everything looking healthy and organised. I remembered his cow in Julia's paddock and should have realised that something was wrong.

We knocked on his door and waited. It appeared he wasn't home, but his town car and his truck were both there, as was his unregistered motorbike, which he used around the farm. We turned to go across to his shed when we heard a quiet voice from inside.

'Who is it?'

Having given our names, he cautiously opened the door. He stood in the doorway with his dressing gown covering his thin body, his thick hair uncombed, and his pale face unshaven. Looking at us warily through sunken, dull eyes, he whispered, 'Hello.'

CHAPTER FORTY-SIX

Marianne pushed the door open and walked in. I was shocked and thought she was rude when she questioned Mr Thomas about what he had been eating and drinking. After all, we had just come to ask about his truck.

She sensed my hesitancy and, turning to me, whispered, 'Louisa, I am a nurse. He is extremely sick.'

I watched as Marianne helped him to a comfortable recliner and checked his vital signs. He had a high fever and was dehydrated, complaining of aches and pains all over. She checked his breathing and assured him that he had a bad flu, but no sign of pneumonia. She asked him when he had last eaten.

'I haven't had the strength to go to town for food over the last few weeks, so I have mainly eaten the eggs from my chickens. It has taken all my strength to feed them and the dogs, and I haven't even been able to check on the cows.'

He was alone with no one to look after him, and no one knew he was very sick. He had no family since his wife died over a year ago. I regret having never taken the time to get to know her in the few months before she died. I had been too caught up in my own little world of pain.

By this time, Marianne and I had forgotten all about the truck.

I was impressed by Marianne's expert care of him and her kindness. He smiled and repeatedly thanked her for helping him. She made him a warm drink and checked his fridge, where she found a bit of butter and cheese and something unrecognisable, covered in mould.

I found some Jatz biscuits and a can of soup, and heated the soup for him while Marianne buttered the biscuits and added some cheese. She gave him a mug of soup and watched him drink it. She planned to leave once he had finished the cheese and biscuits and the soup and had at least one glass of water. We left him in his chair with another glass of water beside him and promised to come back with some groceries within an hour.

I phoned the book club ladies and briefly told them about Mr Thomas's sickness and his need for some meals. I remarked to Brenda that Mr Thomas urgently needed some help with his farm, and she suggested we organise a working bee for the next day, which conveniently was Saturday. We knew if we asked him first, he would have declined our offer, so we decided to go ahead and try to organise it on short notice. We were hopeful that at least a few people could come.

Irene had some chicken casserole left over from the night before, and Terry had some freshly baked chocolate biscuits. When we stopped at the cafe, Brenda said she knew Mr Thomas well as he was a regular customer. She had been concerned that she hadn't seen him for a couple of weeks, and was annoyed with herself for not having checked on him. She had a meat pie, a pastry and some shepherd's pie that she could give him.

I had Marianne stop at my place as I had some fresh bread and some milk, cream and cheese. I also grabbed some bananas and a bunch of grapes.

We drove around the town and collected the food from our friends, with promises of more to come. Everyone we spoke to was keen and available to come and lend a hand the following day. We were over-whelmed by the response and were sure Mr Thomas would be also.

Joanna and her mother had nothing cooked, but planned to have some dinners ready by tomorrow when they came for the working bee. Her mother could not do a lot to help, but Joanna didn't want to leave her home alone and have her miss out on a social gathering and a change of scenery.

We stopped at Charlotte's and I went in to find Jason. I told Charlotte and the children about Mr Thomas, and they were all keen to come to the working bee the following day. They were excited to be able to help someone in need and perhaps take their minds off their loss for a moment. I thought it would do them good to spend the day surrounded by friends.

Karen, David and their boys were also free to help. It was great to have some manpower, as we knew, because of the cow in Julia's paddock, at least one fence needed mending. On our way back to Mr Thomas's, Marianne stopped at the chemist and bought some vitamins, electrolytes and pain pills.

When we arrived with arms full of the goodies, Mr Thomas cried. He was overwhelmed by the kindness and words failed him. We told him we had arranged a working bee for the following day, and asked him to write a list of the urgent jobs. He lowered his eyes and shook his head, still unable to speak.

My heart had been softened, as I no longer saw a recluse but a tired and lonely human being. How fast we can judge people when we don't know the burdens they carry or the pain in their hearts.

Before we left, I fed the dogs and chooks and gathered the eggs. Marianne heated some food for Mr Thomas and gave him some pills and vitamins. She also gave him a drink of water with electrolytes and put another glass of water beside his chair. We could see a change in him already as he was regaining the hope of recovery. Perhaps he was at the point of giving up before we had arrived. I saw the hand of God in the timing of our visit, which left me in awe. I gathered a basketful of washing as we were leaving, and Marianne told him she would be back in the morning to check on him before we all arrived to start work.

We headed into town for a quick lunch before Marianne went home to her husband. I had watched her as she expertly cared for Mr Thomas, and she mentioned while we ate our toasted sandwiches and soup that he may not have survived much longer if we hadn't found him today. He was dangerously dehydrated, which can be fatal in a man with little flesh on his bones.

CHAPTER FORTY-SEVEN

Saturday was another warm spring day. Marianne had checked on Mr Thomas at about eight o'clock and called in to say he was up and looked healthier. He had showered, shaved and dressed and had already fed the chooks and dogs. She couldn't come to the working bee but would drop by when she could to check on him.

The rest of us arrived at about nine, laden with food, tools and cleaning products.

Joanna and her mother must have worked late into the night cooking delicious meals for Mr Thomas. They had six plastic containers with meals that he could freeze and heat when needed, and some desserts and snacks. Brenda brought some salad bowls, sandwiches and cold drinks from her shop for all the workers.

David and his boys started on the fences, checking for places the cows could get out. They found three cows making their way into Julia's paddock, steered them home and mended the fence.

Mr Thomas came outside during our lunch break to thank us, with tears of gratitude flowing uncheck-ed. While he was smothered in hugs, he asked us all to please call him Jack. He vowed to repay us for our kindness when he was fit again, but we assured him it was not necessary.

Dear Jason was in his element, as he followed David around, asking questions and doing what he could to help. He was keen to learn, and I noticed Jack watching him.

Some of us worked inside, cleaning the kitchen and bathrooms and vacuuming the floors. Joanna's mum relaxed, watching us while we worked, having short conversations with Jack, who had been instructed to remain in his armchair. We cleaned windows, floors and cupboards, completing a spring cleaning in a day, while enjoying working together.

David's boys mowed the orchard and pruned the fruit trees. Charlotte's younger children cleaned out the chicken coop and helped weed and water the vegetable garden. Jack hadn't planted the summer vegetables yet, so Charlotte and Karen went to the town nursery and bought some seedlings. They had lettuce, tomatoes, capsicums, cucumbers, and zucchinis planted in neat rows in no time.

Malcolm and David took turns on the tractor ploughing up Jack's back paddock, ready to sow his sorghum crop after the next rain.

David and Karen's sons were skilled with various tools, so were able to mend some loose boards on Jack's front verandah and do some other minor repairs.

We all looked for jobs we could do, with both men and women working inside and out.

By late afternoon, we had used up our energy but were satisfied with what we had accomplished. Above all else, we enjoyed working together and blessing Jack. It was the first time Charlotte's children had met everyone, and they enjoyed helping.

When we were leaving, I saw Jack head over to chat with Jason. By the grin on Jason's face, I knew Jack had asked him if he could come and help him on the farm.

As Terry was about to leave, she said, 'Jack, I would like to drop by one morning a week and do some housework for you.'

He was grateful and said his wife had kept the place spotless and tidy, but since she died, he hadn't managed to keep up the house and the farm. He wanted to pay her, but she scoffed at the idea.

Marianne and I made a point of popping in to see Jack each

morning over the next week, and the change in him was remarkable. Even by the end of the week, he looked healthier and years younger. His energy level had improved daily.

A week after the working bee, when Marianne and I dropped by to check on Jack, he asked, 'Why did you come to my place originally, a week or so ago?'

We looked at each other and laughed as we had both forgotten the favour we wanted to ask him. When we told him about the fair, our idea for a float, and our need for a truck, he volunteered his before we could ask. We asked if he would drive it for us in the parade.

He smiled and, bowing, said, 'It would be an honour.'

Now we had the harder task ahead, of designing our book club float.

CHAPTER FORTY-EIGHT

Brenda possessed exceptional creative talent, although I should have realised it sooner by the way she had decorated her cafe. Joanna had mentioned that she worked for an advertising agency, but we didn't know she was in charge of the creative side and was an artist. We had two talented people on our team.

Brenda took the lead to get us started, 'We need slogans before we start working on our props and decorations, and I'm sure we all want to say something that encourages people to value books and make reading an integral part of their lives.'

We had just a month to get our float together with a limited budget, but plenty of volunteers. Brenda and Joanna could get started, once we decided on the slogans and the rest of us would source the needed materials and follow their instructions.

Karen said, 'Friendship is a big advantage of being in the book club, so maybe we should include that in the message on our slogans. People will remember our catchy slogans after they have forgotten the decorations on our float.'

We planned to put one along each side and the back, and one on top. Joanna and Brenda would work out the most suitable materials to use and how to add the lettering.

They suggested we make book shapes for the top of the float out of chicken wire, and stuff them with newspaper or plastic. The exact style and content of the decorations were left for them to design.

After trips to the thrift shops, and looking through our

home supplies, we accumulated more materials than we needed.

Joanna and Brenda proved to be the perfect creative team. It was interesting to watch them plan, as Joanna seemed to have a calming effect on Brenda, while Brenda was able to build Joanna's confidence and draw out some of her great ideas.

The colours they chose were vivid and rich.

'We think these colours represent our club. It is vibrant and exciting, not dry and boring,' Joanna said.

Along each side of the truck, our slogans were written on plain fabric surrounded by tinsel and mounted on thin boards. Brenda painted the outlines of the letters, and the rest of us had the task of filling them in by sticking on various coloured fabrics. The variety of bright colours made the letters come alive.

Despite being a time-consuming task, it was enjoyable working and laughing together. Joanna made our main slogan, which looked like a bookmark, for the top of the cabin of Jack's truck. 'Book Club, a Novel Way to Bond'.

Brenda shaped chicken wire to look like two giant books and a smaller one, which, under her supervision, we stuffed with recycled newspapers and plastic bags. The quilters then went through their stashes of fabric and found suitable colours to cover the 'books'. David, assisted by his boys, did the carpentry work to put it all together and to make it stable.

Marianne was able to join us as she brought her husband, Alan, along in his wheelchair for two or three hours each day. It was nice for them to have a change of scenery and get to know some of the townsfolk better. Jack wheeled Alan around to look at the animals and machinery, asking Alan for his thoughts on some of his plans and ideas. Jack has a gift of making people feel they have worth, no matter their age or condition. I saw Marianne give Jack a look of gratitude, and Jack winked with a slight nod.

The giant books that Brenda, Joanna, David and his boys constructed were more challenging than anticipated. However, they did a skilful job and the books were eye-catching. Two oversized books were on the tray, and the smaller one was attached to the bonnet of the truck.

Alan asked, 'What will be the titles and authors on the giant books? How about making up some funny ones?'

We loved the idea, having previously thought we would leave them blank. During our break for lunch one day, with Alan's help, we came up with some clever and some funny ones.

"Diary of an AWOL Russian Soldier" by Iza Nikanoff and "Frozen Wastes" by I.C. Miles.

The little book on the bonnet of the truck would read "The Shattered Window" by Bro. Ken Payne.

We needed to put in long hours as the day approached, as the decorating was taking longer than expected. There were also setbacks along the way, although nothing that we were unable to overcome. It turned out to be difficult to make the big books stand up, without the risk of them toppling over, but Jack allowed a few holes to be drilled into the tray of his truck so they could be mounted securely.

This project highlighted the diverse talents within our group, which were not apparent when we came together to discuss books. The bookmarks were in place. On top of the truck's cabin, it read "Book Club - A Novel Way to Bond" and on one side, along the hungry boards, "Come for the Books, Stay for the Friendship". On the opposite side - "We Have All the Best Stories". We especially loved our cheeky one on the back, which had been suggested by Joanna, "We Have Read That Movie".

We had put discarded pieces of carpet on the bed of the truck, which cut down the noise and made it easier to stabilise the chairs and books.

The day before the parade, our beautiful float was ready.

David said, 'Let's take it for a drive, to be certain nothing is going to fall off.'

We were all gathered at Jack's shed, putting on the finishing touches and celebrating the fruit of our labours. Jack climbed into the driver's seat and turned the key, but it would not start.

Jack looked worried. 'I don't understand. Just last week I changed the oil, checked all the hoses, and Jason helped me bleed the brakes. We took her for a spin and she purred like a kitten.'

Soon the bonnet was up, and heads disappeared underneath, trying to find the problem. They checked the battery and all the wiring and found nothing amiss. Discouragement led to despair as the afternoon wore on. If these people couldn't find the problem, all our work would be in vain.

The younger children were playing in the shed beside the truck.

Out of the silence, Charlotte's 8-year-old daughter, Gracie, spoke. 'Maybe it needs petrol.'

Collective gasps and moans were heard. Jack said, 'Jason, grab that jerry can next to my bike, will you?'

Jason ran out of the shed, came back with a jerry can, and poured the petrol into the thirsty tank.

After some fiddling with hoses, Jack again turned the key, and the deep, throaty purr of the engine filled the silence, steady and powerful, almost drowning out our cheers. We will always remember the immense relief that washed over us at that sound.

CHAPTER FORTY-NINE

We were blessed with perfect weather on the Saturday of the fair. The temperature was about 24 degrees, with sunshine and a slight breeze. The town had buzzed with excitement and activity all week as the main street was transformed by vendors setting up their stalls.

We were all proud of our float, and since Terry, Irene and I weren't involved in any stalls, we volunteered to ride on the back, sitting on chairs with books in our hands.

Our float was a moving work of art, bursting with colour and creativity, and I heard claps and shouts of "Wow" as we passed by.

We drove past the high school's 'sausage sizzle' stall where Charlotte and her children were busy taking orders, and they clapped and cheered as we passed. To our surprise, they had sausages and onions stuffed into long, soft bread rolls, waiting for us to come by. Charlotte's 14-year-old son, Patrick, raced over to the float, handed the rolls wrapped in serviettes to the three of us on the back and thrust two through the passenger window to Jack and Jason. We had bottles of water with us to add to our delicious lunch.

This was the first year I participated in the fair, which made it more exciting than the previous year when I had enjoyed the sights and the stalls. I was very new to town then. I felt more like a member of the community, and even Australia, and less like an immigrant this year. Sitting with my friends on the float, enjoying the festive atmosphere and waving to all the people was a thrilling experience. In the midst of it all, my vision became blurred, recalling all the wonderful things that had unfolded since the Spring Fair last year. Terry noticed how moved I was and, leaning forward, smiled and squeezed my hand.

'It has been an amazing year for all of us, hasn't it?' she remarked.

I could only smile and nod.

We travelled through the streets lined with the families and friends of the town, relishing each moment. I scanned the crowd, my eyes darting warily, half-expecting to see Dorjan lurking in the throng. I didn't spot him and concluded he would be busy in his supermarket, as the town was crowded for the fair.

In front of us was a float with members of the primary school choir singing our national anthem, followed by everyone's favourite, 'Waltzing Matilda', a song that made no sense when I first heard it. It is filled with Australian expressions, which had to be explained to me. I joined in enthusiastically with the people lining the streets, thankful that they couldn't hear my croaky voice.

Through the window in the back of the truck's cabin, I watched Jack singing with great enthusiasm, and Jason laughing beside him and also singing along. Those two had become such fast friends. It warmed my heart to see what a gift they were to each other.

The day ended with the traditional fireworks, which we all, without bias, agreed surpassed the New Year's Eve display on the Sydney Harbour Bridge.

Jason and Jack took the truck back to the farm after the parade, fed the animals and returned in Jack's car so he could give Julia, Terry and me a lift home.

I hadn't seen Julia during the day, apart from a wave from the crowd. As the committee chairwoman this year, she had worked tirelessly and was exhausted but content as we lounged together on a blanket on the grass watching the finale of the fireworks.

With a satisfied sigh, she said, 'The fair has been a success and I'm pleased my job is finished for another year. I don't think I will be involved next year.'

I laughed.

Having had such a life-changing year, I was keen to see what lay ahead. Of one thing I was certain, that my involvement in the lives of my friends would be increasing as I planned to do what I could to help them.

CHAPTER FIFTY

The weeks that followed the fair were pleasant ones, full of social events with friends and garden preparation for the coming hot months. Julia and I grow things to share. If I plant cherry tomatoes, she plants the big ones. She will plant two cucumber plants and I will plant two zucchini plants, which is enough for both of us with some to spare. It is not easy to find recipients of our abundant supply of fruit and vegetables during the summer months, as we all have bountiful crops. I often end the summer with several loaves of zucchini bread in the freezer, as I can't throw away food. I am pleased my chickens are willing to eat the extra vegetables too.

Despite all the distractions of preparations for the fair and the summer planting, I spent time pondering my past. The times spent milking are opportunities for reflection. Looking back over my life, I now recognise that the hand of God had guided and protected me. I was alive when friends and relatives died in Auschwitz or the ghettos. I vacillated between gratitude to God and 'survivor's guilt', which I recognise does not come from God.

I'm sticking with gratitude.

I am determined to dedicate my life to serving Him wherever He calls me. I do not consider being sixty-three a hindrance, but am yielding each day I have to Him.

I made myself available to both Marianne and Charlotte to help them in any way possible and was humbled by the effect of my meagre support.

Some days, I made dinner for Charlotte and the children, and I often took a bunch of flowers from my garden and spent time with her when the children were at school. I wasn't attempting to replace dear Rosa but thought I might be able to fill the gap in some small way. Charlotte always appreciated the meals and the break from cooking. Her home was a lively yet organised one, and I was enjoying getting to know all her children. Jason was second in line after Anna, who, at 18, wanted nothing to do with me. When I visited, she was sullen and did not talk to me. I saw the worried look on Charlotte's face as her eyes followed her. After Jason came Patrick, age 14. He is in the awkward adolescent stage, but was a cheerful, talkative youth. Jane, 10, is a bright child who follows Jason around like his shadow and is full of questions, which he patiently answers. The youngest was 8-year-old Grace, who had solved the problem with the truck the day before the fair. She likes to sit with me every moment, if possible, as she misses her Aunty Rosa very much.

Charlotte was doing an amazing job teaching them manners and respect for each other. They all did chores, which helped them appreciate all she did for them. I knew Jason well by this time, and I enjoyed getting acquainted with the rest of the family and fitting them into the various stories Jason had told me.

One evening, I was about to head home after dinner with the family, when Gracie said, 'Grandma, you talk funny. Why don't you talk like us?'

(Gracie had started calling me 'Grandma' like Jason, and I loved it.)

Charlotte gasped, as I laughed.

'That is a great question, Gracie. I try to talk like you, but I am not good at it. The reason is that when I was a little girl like you, I spoke a different language and could not speak one word of English. I had never even heard anyone speak English.'

'I will say something to you in one of my other languages. See if you can understand. Hela Gresi. bist du a gute meydl'

They all laughed, saying that they were not real words. I told them that I said, 'Hello, Gracie. Are you a good girl?'

She couldn't believe that was what I said.

I asked her to please get me a piece of paper so I could write what I had said.

ביסט דו אַ גוטע מיידל .גרעסי העלא

Of course, that was even stranger than hearing it. They had trouble believing that my writing said anything.

Patrick asked me the name of the language, and when I answered, 'Yiddish', there were more giggles.

'We mostly spoke Hungarian, but I had learnt Yiddish from our elderly housekeeper when I was young. It is a Jewish language, similar to Hebrew, that was spoken by Jews in many parts of Europe years ago.'

Charlotte asked me how I learnt English.

'After the war, my mum and I were able to go to Great Britain.

'We decided we couldn't stay in Hungary for a lot of reasons, including the fact that our home and our country were destroyed.

'We arrived there in 1946 and were allowed to stay until we found a country for permanent residence.

'While there, we concentrated on learning English, while working together in a beautiful florist shop. Our English was not good, so we worked in the back of the shop, learning how to make a variety of flower arrangements. We enjoyed working with flowers as we had not seen them for quite some time. There were no flowers to be seen in the city of Budapest after the devastation.'

'Ah,' Charlotte exclaimed. 'That is why you grow such beautiful flowers in your garden and always have colourful arrangements to give away.'

I smiled and told them about the owner of the shop.

'She was a kind older lady, from Finland, and her name was Elina Jarvella. She brought healing to us, and because of her kindness, we felt we could start to live again. She knew how it felt to be in a foreign country with an unfamiliar culture and language, so she was patient with us and helped us with our English. She also had a good understanding of how the Jewish people in Europe suffered throughout the terrible war, as she had met refugees in her shop and heard their stories. I will always remember that sweet lady as she allowed us to live above the shop and charged us no rent. For a long time, we had not experienced kindness as Jews, as there had been unreasonable restrictions placed on us in Hungary. At first, we were suspicious of her, and it took us a while to become confident that she wouldn't steal from us or do us harm.'

I kept sending her postcards of different places in Australia for quite a few years. She would send postcards back to us showing various places in Britain. I was very sad several years ago when her postcards stopped coming, and I had one of mine come back stamped with 'Return to Sender'. She was older than my mother, so I assumed she had died.

'How did you end up coming from Britain to Australia?' Charlotte asked.

We heard that Australia had a 'Populate or Perish' policy, which in 1948, resulted in assisted immigration being extended to Europeans, instead of just the British, and we were thrilled to be part of it.

Australia did not accept Hungarians straight after the war, as we were considered former enemies. This policy was reversed in the middle of 1948, and about seventeen thousand Hungarians came to Australia over the next five years.

We had an interview and were accepted to travel here.'

Patrick sweetly said, "And we are all glad you did.'

After several hugs, I headed home.

CHAPTER FIFTY-ONE

In contrast to the constant activity in Charlotte's home, I visited Marianne and Alan's quiet house at least once a week and came to enjoy getting to know them too. Alan wanted to hear more details of my experiences in Hungary, which I found easy to share since writing my letter. We spent hours talking, often while Marianne went out for coffee or did her shopping. I found it relaxing talking with both of them. Alan, a gifted teacher, explained passages of the Bible to me that I found confusing. Marianne told me that he enjoyed my questions.

Alan had read widely about what happened in Auschwitz, including when rail trucks became available. Budapest Jews were also deported to Auschwitz for gassing and the crematorium, or labour camps and probable death by starvation. Hundreds were also used in cruel experiments.

He shared something horrific that he had read. 'When they took the people towards the gas chamber, they told them to strip off, as they were going to have showers. The guards instructed them to put their clothes on numbered hooks and to memorise the number so they could find their clothes after their shower. They delighted in deceiving these innocent people as they led them to their deaths. They were herded into a room holding over 1,600 people packed close together. To continue the deception, they even put fake shower heads on the ceiling, and then poured in the poisonous gas crystals from above. The fumes burnt the people's lungs, and their bodies convulsed as if they were having seizures.'

I didn't say anything as the faces of lost friends and family scrolled through my mind, including those of little children.

Alan had also read about the deportations starting on May 15, 1944, and how over the following fifty-five days, the Nazis deported almost half a million Jews from Hungary by train to Auschwitz. Tens of thousands arrived each day, and the majority were killed soon after arrival.

I told him this had been carried out with the assistance of departments in our own government and military police, with members closely linked to the Arrow Cross, the evil Hungarian party.

Thousands of prominent Hungarian Jews disappeared as soon as Hungary was occupied and were tortured and killed by the Gestapo.

He said he found the statistics shocking, as of about 825,000 Jews living in Hungary in 1941, about sixty-three thousand died or were killed before the German occupation of early 1944. Under German occupation, more than five hundred thousand died from maltreatment or were murdered.

Some two hundred and fifty thousand Jews survived the Holocaust, which is less than one-third of those who had lived in Hungary in March 1944. I told Alan about the heroes of the war, as I knew he would enjoy doing further research on these brave men.

'After the railways and trains had been bombed, German soldiers forced Jews to walk over three hundred kilometres in the snow to the border with Austria to be taken to Auschwitz. Even though a large number died or were shot along the way, Swedish dignitaries, including Dr Shendor Unger, Raoul Wallenberg and Per Anger, rescued about five hundred Jews. They arrived with vans and called out names. They told the people they had 'left behind' their papers and were under the protection of the Swedish Government. Fortunately, most of the Arrow Cross and German soldiers were illiterate and were impressed by any document that had a stamp on it.

'Alan, these men then took the people they rescued to safe houses that they had set up in Hungary under the protection of the Swedish government.

'They could have been safe at home in Sweden, but instead risked their lives daily to rescue as many Jews as possible.

'The scheme was conceived by a lesser-known man called Miklos Moshe Krausz, who had run the Jewish Agency's Budapest office to facilitate the immigration of Hungarian Jews to Israel. Soon after Germany invaded Hungary, Krausz changed to rescuing Jews. He was a man who did not seek any recognition for saving thousands of his fellow Jews.

'There are varying estimates as to the number rescued during the war. We do know there were thousands, with rescues carried out by foreigners sympathetic to the Jews, as well as members of the Hungarian Zionist Youth.

'This next part of the story is truly amazing. Wallenberg was such a brave man. In January 1945, he learned of a German plan to murder the remaining Jews in the Budapest ghettos. He sent a note to the commander of the German forces in Hungary, stating that should a massacre take place, he would be held personally responsible and probably be tried and executed as a war criminal at the end of the war. The planned liquidation was cancelled, and just two days later, Budapest was liberated by Soviet forces. Through this action, Wallenberg was responsible for saving over one hundred thousand lives.

'He risked his own life arguing and fighting the German SS and the Arrow Cross gangs, even though these men were trigger-happy and dangerous.

'Wallenberg issued passports to anyone who required protection. He was a real hero – he fought without weapons, without even a belief in God or religion, but as a compassionate human being. He paid for it all, losing his freedom and his life.'

'Why, what happened to him?' Alan asked.

'He was arrested by the Soviets after the war and disappeared, presumably dying in a Soviet prison. Since then, he has been recognised and honoured by several countries.

He must never be forgotten.'

I continued, 'Carl Lutz was also responsible for saving tens of thousands of Jews from deportation or death by issuing and distributing protective passes, which made it possible for thousands of Jews to emigrate to Israel. He also set up safe houses, including the Glass House, where my mother and I stayed. He offered protection and shelter to thousands of Jews between 1944 and the liberation of Budapest in January 1945.'

Alan assured me that he planned to find out all he could about these brave men. He said he had read that the Germans even killed children and little babies.

Marianne was shocked. 'How could they do that?? These children and babies could do them no harm.'

I explained to them that the soldiers believed the babies and children deserved to die because they had Jewish blood. If allowed to live, they would grow into Jewish adults who were as much of a pest as rats.

Marianne asked, 'How could people ever be indoctrinated to the point that they could believe such a lie?

'Slowly,' I said.

'The newspapers and magazines began their campaign of antisemitism by feeding unbelievable rubbish to their readers. Jews were described as monsters who killed Gentile children to use their blood in the unleavened bread of their Passover. The newspapers announced that Jews raped blonde girls and murdered them as part of their religious practices.

'The war and the shortages of materials and food were all said to be caused by the Jews directed by Churchill and Roosevelt, who were falsely said to be Jewish. Although not Jewish, both were sympathetic to the Jews.

'The German soldiers, and even our fellow Hungarians, were brainwashed into thinking that Jews were an inferior race and therefore should be exterminated. They were taught in school that we Jews were all sneaky potential rapists and murderers. Some children's books were written displaying Jews in this way. Children grew up being taught to hate us and that Jews were a constant danger and caused great pain to the world, often lurking in the shadows. The German soldiers were trained to be ruthless and heartless. They had been told that we were not fit to live, and treated us accordingly.

'We heard that the soldiers marched in the streets of Hungarian-occupied territories, like Transylvania, singing songs with a chorus of, "Dirty Jews, stinking Jews, go to Palestine." The pro-Nazi government kept referring to "The Jewish Problem", and anti-Jewish propaganda even came from leaders of the church.'

I always enjoyed my time with Alan and Marianne, and although they often asked me about my painful past, I always felt relaxed with them.

However, there was one day that I visited Marianne and Alan that caused me much discomfort.

CHAPTER FIFTY-TWO

On one of my visits, Alan, Marianne and I discussed 'The Lord's Prayer', the answer Jesus gave the disciples when they had asked Him how to pray. We read the verse after it in Matthew 6. Jesus said if we don't forgive others, our heavenly Father won't forgive us. Shocked, I kept shifting in my chair and then paced around the room. Alan challenged me with something deep inside I had known for some time.

'Louisa, you must forgive Dorjan Halmi.'

I spun around and almost shouted, 'Alan, no. You know what he did. Not to my family alone, but he sent hundreds, if not thousands, of innocent people to a cruel death.'

Alan answered calmly. 'Louisa, you know I am right. Even without this verse, you know that you must.'

He was right. I knew I had to, as the Lord had forgiven me, but I could not do it, so I tried to convince Alan and Marianne that it was not necessary.

Marianne then hugged me and whispered, 'I saw you at Rosa's funeral. I saw you catch a glimpse of Dorjan and run from the building. I followed you and watched you run into the bushes, so I went inside and found Julia. We didn't expect Dorjan to come to the funeral, but I want you to know that the Lord has touched his heart too. He is not the same man he was in Hungary.'

My heart was racing, as my stomach churned. 'It doesn't matter,' I said, 'It doesn't make any difference. He was a heartless murderer. Nothing will bring those people back. He doesn't deserve to be forgiven.'

Alan agreed. 'Yes, that is true, Louisa. But we are not thinking about them or him. We are thinking about you.'

He motioned towards my chair, saying, 'Sit down, Louisa, and let's talk.'

He smiled at Marianne and added, 'We have a story to share with you.'

I forced myself to calm down and soon sat again, as Marianne placed another cup of tea in my hand. I wanted to hear their story, but I was guarded, ready to defend my position.

But their story was beyond anything I expected to hear.

Alan and Marianne then described the battle they had with forgiving. Their son, Peter, at sixteen, was killed by a youth who, while driving in a drug-controlled state, swerved at high speed and killed their boy as he was walking his dog. I had noticed pictures of two teenagers on their mantlepiece and had assumed one was their son. Marianne took one down and showed me the last picture taken of Peter.

They said how bitter and angry they had felt and how they had hoped the irresponsible youth would spend the rest of his life in gaol.

I nodded in agreement, saying, 'He deserved no less. I hope he is still rotting in a cell.'

They smiled and explained how soon they realised that their anger and bitterness were harming themselves and their relationship with God.

Alan explained, 'Unforgiveness is like drinking poison and hoping the other person dies. We realised we were poisoning ourselves.'

When they cried out to the Lord for help, He gave them both a heart of compassion for the boy. They knew that he had to live the rest of his life with the guilt and shame of what he had done. They asked the Lord to give them the strength to forgive him, as they couldn't do it without the Lord's help. They soon realised that they needed to put their faith into action, so they visited the young man in prison. Marianne said his name is Kevin, and after three years in prison, he is now twenty.

'What happened when you saw him? Did you yell at him at all? Tell him what an idiotic fool he was?'

Alan smiled. 'Marianne and I were nervous and leaned on the Lord for His strength. We were escorted into a room and saw he was more nervous than we were, as he expected at least a terrible tongue-lashing from us.'

Chuckling, Marianne added, 'There were two guards with him instead of the usual one, in case we became violent. That was the furthest thing from our minds, but I guess the guards had seen that sort of thing happen before. They were suspicious as to why we wanted to see him.'

Alan added, 'We wanted above all for him to know we had forgiven him. We no longer felt anger, but were filled with God's deep love for him.

'He responded to our love with agonised wailing and gut-wrenching sobs. The pain he had borne gushed out of every pore. Our hearts were breaking, and the guards broke the rules, allowing us to hold him as he cried.'

Marianne and Alan became teary recalling that day as if it were yesterday. I was choking back tears too.

Over time, they have learnt his story. Kevin had been in foster care all his life, moved from family to family and never belonging anywhere. His experience was tragically the opposite of Karen's. No one wanted him, loved him or cared about him. Drugs and alcohol were used to ease his pain and to escape from a harsh, cold world.

Marianne then went to the mantlepiece and handed me the picture of a handsome, dark-haired young man. She smiled at Alan as she said, 'This is our Kevin.'

I was stunned. They then told me that they now visit him often and take him treats and books to read. He is being trained in carpentry and has shown unusual skill and creativity. They talked about Kevin as though they were his proud parents.

They have appealed his sentence and are praying that he will be released into their custody soon. Kevin is not known in Wattle Creek, which would give him the opportunity to start afresh with a new, responsible and productive life.

I couldn't imagine such a thing was possible, but they assured me it was all God's doing.

'Now, back to you, Louisa,' Alan smiled. 'You have heard what is possible with our Lord.'

'So, you think Dorjan and I will instantly be mates, do you?' I was not happy.

Marianne and Alan laughed.

Marianne explained that they did not expect this outcome from meeting Kevin. Their focus was on forgiving him for their own sake, as they needed peace.

They assured me they were not trying to push me to do anything, but suggested I pray about it and ask the Lord for His guidance. I promised to, and left that day filled with dread, trying hard to convince myself that seeing Dorjan and forgiving him would not be necessary.

'Maybe someday I will write him a letter,' I said to myself as I drove home.

I decided to talk with Julia, thinking she understood how impossible it would be for me to see Dorjan and talk to him. I expected her to agree with me, assuring me that it was not necessary. She'd have my back, and shield me from ever having to see him. Maybe he would soon leave town, and that would be the end of it. I still clung to that hope.

It surprised me that Julia had never offered information about her young years. Although we have been neighbours and best friends for most of our adult lives, I realised that she had not shared details of her early life with me. We had enjoyed day-to-day life together, but neither of us had opened up about our pasts. When I was forced to reveal mine, Julia didn't even crack the door open to give me a glimpse into her earlier years, and I did not intend to force my way in. Perhaps they had been uneventful.

I didn't realise that Julia would open that door herself.

CHAPTER FIFTY-THREE

Julia came to dinner and we settled in for a chat over the roast lamb and chocolate ice cream I hadn't ordered. I explained how Marianne and Alan were encouraging me to visit Dorjan. I related what they had shared, without including their story about Kevin, but I emphasised that I didn't expect her to agree with them.

She was silent and looked uncomfortable, with her eyes focused on her food, moving the vegetables around on her plate and not eating anything.

She was struggling with something, so I kept quiet, waiting for her to break the silence.

With a deep sigh, she started, 'I want to give you Dorjan's perspective. I have talked with him, and he is looking for the opportunity to ask you for your forgiveness. He is wise enough to wait and not to put you in a difficult position.

'I have a story I need to tell you, and it is not easy to share, but I know now is the right time.'

She took another deep breath and began.

'Do you remember the book we did a while ago called *Bit by Bit*'?

'Yes,' I said. 'The story of a thief.'

Raising her eyes to look into mine, she whispered, 'That was me, Louisa. That book could have been written about me.'

I caught myself gaping and quickly snapped my mouth shut.

'Do you remember me mentioning an aunt to you? I used

to go with her to church sometimes when I was young. I stole money from her. A LOT of money. My aunt was a wealthy single lady, and I was a gambler. I was a teenager, but I had some 'friends' who introduced me to gambling on horse races. They could place my bets without anyone knowing my age. I had a little money and lost it fast. But I had been bitten by the gambling demon and couldn't stop, so I needed a source of money. My aunt was visiting my parents, and I overheard a conversation where they were joking about PINs and bankcards. They were quite new back then. My aunt mentioned with a laugh that she had made hers simple - 9999. I then realised I only needed her card, and I was set. When she visited, she always left her handbag on the hall table near the front door. I often had an opportunity to grab her bag, find her bankcard and head to the local ATM. It sickens me whenever I think about what I did.'

Julia paused as she relived those days.

'I started taking small amounts out of her account, which I was sure she wouldn't notice. But I became bolder and greedier, as I continued to lose the money that I placed on horses, but I couldn't stop, always believing the next one would be a winner. Her accountant wasn't inclined to want receipts for every cash withdrawal, but questioned her when the amounts became large. My aunt was shocked to discover someone was stealing from her. Her account was closed, another one opened, and a new card issued. That was the end of my source of money. I did not confess as I thought no one suspected me. When I met Jesus, I knew I had to tell her what I had done and ask her forgiveness. I was overwhelmed by anxiety and couldn't find a moment of peace.'

'Did you confess to your aunt?'

'Yes, I did, and it was the hardest thing I have ever done. I loved my aunt, and was terrified of her rejection, although I would not have blamed her for being angry, and even having me arrested.

'She lived in a nursing home by this time, and I often

visited her. When I walked in, determined to confess, she saw my face and knew something was wrong. I blurted out every shameful detail to her through tears and with my voice shaking like leaves in the wind. She sat still, listening, then I held my breath, waiting for the explosion.'

'What happened then, Julia? Did she explode in shock and horror, as you expected? You are not in gaol!'

'My aunt smiled then exclaimed, 'At last. At last. I always knew it was you. It was easy to trace where and when the money had been withdrawn. You were not sneaky enough to withdraw the money far from home. I forgave you years ago, Julia. I have been longing and praying for this day.'

Julia told me the joy on her aunt's face was beautiful and, if possible, she would have leapt out of her wheelchair and danced.

'My aunt's reaction was beyond my wildest dreams, Louisa. I expected anger, hatred, a sound tongue lashing and for her to either call the police or say she never wanted to see me again.

'I cannot explain what her love and forgiveness did for me. I cried over the next several days, remembering the mercy that she extended to me. I felt like my life had been 'on hold' up until that day, and after receiving her forgiveness, I could live again!'

I knew she wanted to tell me this story to explain the effect of her aunt's forgiveness, and encourage me to extend the same to Dorjan, but I couldn't get past the thought that he didn't deserve it. As if reading my thoughts, she added, 'It's not about deserving it, but about the wonderful blessing it is to both the forgiver and the forgiven.' She said if her aunt had reacted as she had expected, which might be what Dorjan is expecting, she still would have felt free after confessing, but her aunt's kindness brought her unexpected joy. It had been hard for Julia to share such a humbling experience, but she did it out of love for me.

She smiled and reminded me of a story told by Jesus in the Bible about a man who owed what amounted to two thousand years' worth of wages to the king. The king commanded that he and his whole family be sold as slaves to repay the debt. The man begged for time to pay and for the king to be patient. Even though this was a ridiculous request, as he could never repay the debt, the king showed compassion and forgave him the full amount. However, this forgiven man found a man who owed him about eighteen dollars. This debtor begged him to have patience with him, but he refused and had him put into prison. The man had been forgiven thousands of years of wages and could not forgive a little debt. When the king heard about this, he had the heartless man thrown into prison for not being willing to forgive a small amount when he had been forgiven so much.

I had read this story in the Book of Matthew, but didn't understand it until Julia explained it. We are the ones who have been forgiven by our sinless Jesus, and how terrible it is if we are not prepared to forgive our fellow man. No forgiveness that we can offer anyone compares to the forgiveness we have received from Jesus.

My friends were urging me to take a path I was reluctant to follow—yet deep down, I knew it was one I would eventually have to walk.

CHAPTER FIFTY-FOUR

I had trouble sleeping for several nights, trying to convince myself that talking to Dorjan was un-necessary. Those days and nights were tiring without the peace I had enjoyed. I knew it would not return while I was putting my own will ahead of Jesus' command. I saw no way to get relief except obedience.

I talked to Terry about forgiveness and asked if she ever had to do it, apart from having to forgive me.

She laughed, 'Of course. Yes, yes!

'Everyone has the opportunity to extend forgiveness to someone at some point. However, many people never do it, not realising what a liberating experience it is. Those who refuse to forgive can feel tormented, and never find peace. There are many Scriptures that tell us we must forgive others, as we have been forgiven so much. If we want God's forgiveness we must forgive too. One example is just after the Lord answered the disciples question when they asked Him how to pray in Matthew 6.

She encouraged me to go to the supermarket and meet Dorjan when I felt ready.

On the following Wednesday, I decided I had the strength and the right heart attitude to go, confident he wouldn't recognise me as he hadn't known me well during the war.

I walked to the supermarket around noon. Warm, sunny days always lift my mood, so I enjoyed the walk despite the tension in my body. I knew I was walking slower than usual, trying to delay what lay ahead, but facing my fear required me, at this point, to just put one foot in front of the other.

I walked into the supermarket and saw him at the checkout.

My reaction was under better control than when I had unexpectedly seen him at the funeral. I had steeled myself for this moment and calmly walked past him, my eyes averted, to pick up a bag of apples and some bananas. Taking a deep breath, I headed to the checkout. To my surprise, Dorjan had been replaced by a girl I didn't recognise.

I made my purchases and left, elated and disappointed. Perhaps this wasn't God's timing, or maybe He didn't require me to meet Dorjan at all.

Walking home, I convinced myself that a meeting was not necessary.

I spent the afternoon with Terry and shared what I had attempted to do. I believed it was not God's will for me to see Dorjan, and suggested that someday someone could take him a message from me. I don't think I convinced her, but she smiled and suggested that to take my mind off Dorjan, we could go and visit Jack and see if we could do something to help him.

When we arrived, Jack's old motorbike was gone, so we knew he must have been somewhere on the property. We sat on his verandah to wait a while to see if he returned. Terry mentioned she had come to know Jack better while she had cleaned his house, and they were becoming close friends. This was new territory for her, so she was being cautious.

She told me a bit about his wife, whose picture is in every room of his house. They had a beautiful marriage, and her sudden death due to aggressive cancer, had left his ship without a rudder. Over the past year, he had let his life fall into disrepair — his farm, his house and even his health. Since the God-ordained day that Marianne and I knocked on his door, his life has been getting back on course. His farm looked 'alive' again, and the house was neat and clean.

We saw him approaching and, even from a distance, he looked like a changed man. There had been a great improvement in his health, even since the fair the previous month. He had put on a healthy amount of weight, and his face looked years younger than when he had been sick.

He leapt off his bike, full of energy and hurried towards us, pleased with our surprise visit.

Terry had brought some granola bars, and Jack went inside and brought out fresh cups of steaming tea, which we enjoyed while munching on the nutty bars.

Jack said, 'I am more grateful than I can say for all the help I have received. I am convinced that you all saved my life, and not just physically. I had been on a dangerous downward spiral but had no inclination or energy to pull myself out of it.'

He added, 'I uttered a half-hearted prayer, asking God, if He was there, to help me. My prayer had been heard and answered the day you arrived, so now I am considering the possibility of there being a God who cares.'

He said he enjoyed Jason's energetic and enthusiastic company.

'He comes by on Saturdays after milking Bessie and having breakfast with you, Louisa. Together we have sprayed the fruit trees and weeded the vegetable garden. I have taught Jason how to mend a fence and check on the cows.'

Laughing, he added, 'I have even taught him how to kill and pluck a chicken. He proudly took the one he had killed and plucked himself home for Charlotte to cook.'

They had worked together planting the sorghum crop, which was coming up beautifully.

'Jason had been thrilled to learn how to drive the tractor. I have also taught him some basic mechanics when my temperamental motorbike had problems. I enjoy his company as well as his enthusiasm. He is a willing pupil and a joy to have around.'

As we were leaving, Jack said with a wink, 'I have a surprise for Jason at Christmas and no amount of pleading from you two can coax it out of me.'

Of course, we were going to try.

I went home with a cheerful heart, but still with an uneasy feeling I tried to ignore.

CHAPTER FIFTY-FIVE

Despite my resolution to avoid the supermarket, I had no peace. Terry and I spent an enjoyable hour with Jack, but when I thought of Dorjan again, I felt unsettled once more. I could no longer turn away from what I knew was vital, not only for my own healing, as Alan and Marianne had shown me, but for Dorjan's too. I had to look him in the eye and release him with forgiveness.

Perhaps I should have enlisted some prayer support, but instead, I decided this was something I wished to do on my own. Just me and Jesus. I walked boldly back to the supermarket three days later, following the same routine. Dorjan was at the check-out serving a customer, so he did not see me walk in. I wandered aimlessly through the supermarket for several minutes, looking at things I had no interest in buying. I picked up some biscuits that I didn't need, and taking a deep breath, made my way to the checkout, and placed them on the counter. This time, when I saw Dorjan there, I looked at him and spoke in Hungarian.

'Helló, Dorjan, a nevem Balint Lilla.'

He softly replied, also in our native tongue, avoiding eye contact with me, 'Thank you for coming to see me, Lilla.'

I said nothing, and after an awkward silence, he continued.

'David from the church, came to tell me that you lived here, that he knew about our relationship in Hungary, and that you had heard that I was the new manager of the supermarket. I was as shocked to know you were here in remote Wattle Creek, as I know you were to hear of my arrival. Of course, I had no idea you were in Australia, and I am sure I am the last person you would want to see here. I don't blame you for staying away from the supermarket.

'David told me about a month ago that you also had come to know Jesus, and hoped that one day I could ask for your forgiveness, and express my deep regret for the suffering I caused you and your family. I told him that I would not go to you, but would wait until you were ready to see me. I expected that it could take a very long time.'

Without looking at me, he added quietly, 'I desperately want to ask for your forgiveness, knowing I don't deserve it and am not expecting it. But I need to ask for it anyway, and tell you how deeply I regret my cruelty to you, Asher, your mother and so many others.

'The torture I have endured in the years since the war has been no less than I deserved. I couldn't sleep, Lilla. I dreaded the nights. Faces haunted me, especially in the darkness. I kept hearing the weeping and the screams. But I deserved this torture, the hell I was living, and much more. I was disgusted by the wild beast I had been in those war years. My friends and I became blood-thirsty animals, laughing at the pain we inflicted.

'I thought moving to Australia would wipe away the memories, but they followed me here. Moving to Wattle Creek was another attempt to run from my past.

'I had been searching for relief from my torment, and, out of desperation, I visited the church. I had not been inside one before, as we were taught that religion was for deluded, weak people.

'David saw me and came and sat with me while I cried. He stayed, listened and talked with me for a very long time. He showed he cared, although he didn't know me.

'I told him to leave, as he didn't know who I was or what I had done. He smiled at me and told me he was staying. I thought I knew how to get him to leave me alone, so I began to tell him horrific things I had done, but he didn't flinch. He had his arm around me and he didn't remove it, no matter how depraved and disgusting the deeds I confessed. I felt more repulsed telling him, than showed on his face. His eyes never lost their tenderness. I tried harder to disgust him, but he didn't change. I thought he must have been deaf.

'He told me I could have my sins washed away, but I was certain he wouldn't say that if he had been listening.

'I felt drawn back to that building night after night. I knew it was just bricks and mortar, but I felt a Presence there. Often David would come and sit with me. Sometimes, as I cried, he would tell me again what Jesus had done, and how His arms were open wide to me. Other times he would sit silently, his arms wrapped around me and cry with me. I have since read in the Bible a verse that says to weep with those who weep, but I found his tears hard to endure. I didn't understand why he cared about me.

'One night I looked at him and said, "He is real isn't He. You know Him don't you. I see Him in you." Finally, I understood the truth of what David had been telling me, but not only because of his words but also because of his actions. It was that night that I bowed my knee and accepted Jesus' sacrifice for my horrific, vile sins.

'The day I repented and was baptised was the most life changing, freeing day of my life, Lilla. I felt Jesus wash away the sins of the dirtiest person alive, and I truly entered into a new life. For several minutes I hugged David as we both rejoiced. I then grabbed my head and bent over sobbing. David started praying for me, and said later that he thought I was in terrible pain. When I could finally talk, I said, "David. They are gone. The faces, the screaming, the weeping. It has gone! I am free!!" Lilla, Jesus didn't only wash away my sins but He also took away both the eternal punishment I deserve, and the present punishment that the devil was using to torture me night and day.'

With eyes overflowing, Dorjan pleaded, 'Can you ever find a way to forgive me for my heartless cruelty, Lilla? I don't blame you if you can't, but I want you to know how much I regret and have suffered much torment because of the unthinkable things that I did.'

No other customers entered the shop, as I leaned on the counter for support. By the power of the Lord, I extended my hand to him and said, 'I forgive you, Dorjan. I forgive you for what you did to Asher and what you did to my mother and me. As you know, my mother and I survived.'

He nodded, avoiding eye contact.

I assumed he knew that Asher was gone. Since the war, I had longed to hear what happened to Asher after he was forced into Dorjan's van. Now standing before the man with the answers, I knew I would never ask.

He wanted to hear how we managed to survive, and I just whispered, 'Pinchas Rosenbaum.'

He sighed, nodding again, his head bowed.

Never before had I seen a man so broken, as if his body and soul were breaking apart. He clutched my hand, weeping, as a dam of shame, pain and sorrow burst within him. My tears were also flowing like a river breaking its banks. I don't know how long we both stood like this, as no one entered the shop, undoubtedly by God's design.

Much later, still holding my hand, he looked into my eyes. 'I am very sorry, Lilla. So extremely sorry. If I could only go back and live a different life.'

'I understand,' I replied. 'I also have deep regrets. The past cannot be changed, no matter how much we yearn for it. We have the present and we have the future, and that needs to be our focus.'

I realised at that moment how my eyes had recently turned to focus solely on the past, which had robbed me of the joys of the present, as I was fixating on things that could never be changed.

'This is such a beautiful town, Lilla, the people are kind, and I love this job. I have worked in Sydney in the corporate world but wanted to spend my latter years, after the death of my wife, in a less stressful occupation. When I saw this business advertised, I felt it would fit me perfectly. However, when I found out you were here, I wanted to leave. My past, which I always tried to escape, had caught up with me.'

'How did you find out I lived here since I had changed my name?'

'It was about two weeks after my repentance, that David came to see me at my home with your letter in his hand. He told me that you had come from Hungary and had changed your name. He showed me what you had written about me; all true, but you do not know the worst, and I hope you never will.'

His eyes overflowed again.

'David knew most of my wicked past, and even though I had not told him about you and Asher, after reading your letter, he still smiled and hugged me.

'I was devastated, and I planned to leave, although David urged me to stay. With my terrible past now in writing, I expected the townspeople to turn against me and possibly run me out of town. But I had nowhere to go as, instead of becoming an employee, I had bought this business. I couldn't run and I couldn't hide, and I knew my presence here caused you pain.'

I assured him that just a few people had read about him, and they were all sworn to secrecy. This information would not spread all over town.

Dorjan then added that he feels he needs to tell me his story someday, but it is extremely painful for him to look back into that darkness. He said he especially wanted to tell me more about what Jesus had done and was continuing to do in his heart. When the time is right, I know he will share it.

We both stood with hands clasped for a while, savouring the moment as the Lord healed something deep inside both of us. No one can reach out and forgive at this level, except by the power of the Holy Spirit. To stretch out one hand in forgiveness is a small step physically, but a giant leap spiritually. Sorry, Neil Armstrong — your small step on the moon doesn't compare.

A comfortable silence followed, and we ended this time together with a healing hug. With biscuits in hand, as I turned to leave the shop, I looked back at Dorjan and said sheepishly with a smile, 'Thank you for the extra groceries in my orders. You have shown kindness to such an undeserving old lady.'

Through his tears, smiling, he replied in Hungarian, 'You are most welcome, Lilla. And no, you are not undeserving. You have a soft heart. Otherwise, you wouldn't have come today. You deserve infinitely more than I can ever give.'

As I turned and walked out of the shop, I knew something had changed deep inside. A weight that I wasn't aware was so heavy, had been lifted off me. I have heard that heaven rejoices when a soul comes to Jesus for forgiveness, but I'm sure heaven also rejoices when we forgive each other. The power of the forgiveness we receive from Jesus is beyond words, but there seems to be another dimension of peace and healing released when we forgive those who have wronged us. I experienced it that day, and I know Dorjan did too.

It was done. My Lord had gently lifted me over my biggest hurdle, and I was sure Dorjan had experienced the same. The burden of hatred, bitterness and unforgiveness I had carried for over forty years had been removed. This joy and lightness were similar to the joy and peace I received on the day Jesus Himself forgave even me.

The Lord of course knew how important it was for both Dorjan and I to meet up again and for repentance and forgiveness to flow. He was the one who orchestrated for us both to end up in this remote town in Australia, far removed from our former lives in Hungary. I was overwhelmed by His mercy, love and compassion for two seemingly insignificant people, when He has the charge of the whole universe and billions of people. And yet, He cared this much for two old hurting people.

I could never have imagined that the cruel cold-hearted

young man I knew in Hungary could be transformed into the tender-hearted man I just met in the supermarket.

My soul wanted my 63-year-old body to dance and skip all the way home. I felt as light as a helium-filled balloon but filled instead with peace and joy.

I stopped at Julia's to tell her what had happened. I thumped on her door in such an urgent manner that, yet again, I frightened her. She came to the door wide-eyed.

'What has happened??' She asked, with dread clouding her face.

'Nothing bad, nothing bad.' I smiled, catching my breath.

'Come in and tell me. Why are you flustered?'

I told her I had met with Dorjan and how the Lord met with us both. She was overjoyed by the news. We had both sensed a dark cloud had been silent but menacing on our horizons, but now the sky was a brilliant blue again.

Laughter and thanks to the Lord followed. Forgiveness is not just powerful but life-changing. I didn't know it could be like this. I was determined to forgive all who had ever wronged me, alive or dead, including my parents. I wish they had known this power in their own lives.

It was only when I arrived home from Julia's, I realised I didn't pay for the biscuits.

CHAPTER FIFTY-SIX

Since Rosa's funeral, I became curious about the Christian church. The building and the atmosphere had not been what I expected. I had seen Christian churches in movies and pictures as cold and silent, with ministers or priests frowning and telling the people about God's anger.

At the funeral, the atmosphere had been warm and friendly, but I wondered what it was like for a Sunday service. But I couldn't have gone before, knowing Dorjan might be there. With the freedom I was experiencing and having made peace with him, I felt ready to venture in. I didn't expect Dorjan and I to become close friends, but I felt I could see him at the supermarket and the church now without any apprehension, which was indeed a miracle.

When I entered the room, surprise flickered across several faces, including Karen's and David's, before melting into welcoming smiles.

Alan and Marianne were delighted to see me, as, without a word, they knew what I had done. I went and sat beside them, smiled and winked.

The service was not what I expected. The songs were modern, with the words on an overhead projector instead of songbooks. None were familiar to me, but the tunes were easy to follow.

I saw Dorjan seated a few rows in front of us on the opposite side of the church. During the singing, I noticed him constantly wiping his eyes. I remembered reading how Jesus said those who have been forgiven much, love much. The sweet softness in Dorjan came from the great love that he now has for his Saviour. Although he has experienced forgiveness, he still carries a heavy burden of regret. I also have regrets, as we all do, so I prayed for him, as I watched his tears flow.

After the songs, David stood and preached for about half an hour. I couldn't follow it all, but I did hear some beautiful words of Jesus from the Bible in Matthew 11. 'Come to me, all you who are weary and burdened, and I will give you rest. Take my yoke upon you and learn from me, for I am gentle and humble in heart, and you will find rest for your souls. For my yoke is easy and my burden is light.'

David explained how yokes were used on oxen in Jesus' day, and still today in some parts of the world. Mature, experienced oxen have a young ox yoked to them, and they teach them how to pull the plough or cart. The yoke was made so that if the young ox tried to pull in the wrong direction, it would hurt its neck. He told us that young oxen had sore necks before they learned to follow the lead of the older, wiser ox. The analogy became clear as I realised my resistance to forgiving Dorjan had been my way of resisting the direction of Jesus' yoke, and it had been painful.

I felt a connection with the others who were listening to David, as we all wanted to walk with Jesus and honour Him with our lives.

I had asked David once about becoming a member of the church, and if I had to be a member to be part of the body of Christ.

He said, 'You became a member when you accepted that Jesus had died and rose again to pay for your sins, were baptised, and He became your Lord. That is the membership that matters.'

Someone had told me they had become a member of another local church and were given a piece of paper that proved it, but David assured me that was not something he saw in the scriptures, so he didn't do it. I then understood that our bond with believers is because we are all part of His family, not because we attend a particular church building.

I had another challenge that I expected to face soon. My son, daughter and their families were coming to visit over the Christmas period. I hoped to explain the changes that had taken place in my life. I had read in the Bible that Jesus told us not to worry about what we should say, but to trust Him to give us the words. I still felt anxious about it and hoped they might see changes in me. I knew I had changed because of the work Jesus had begun inside me, and I wanted it to be evident to them too. When an unbeliever sees someone changed by God, they cannot easily dismiss it.

I felt ashamed that I had hidden from my children their Hebrew roots and did not introduce them even to the God of the Hebrew Bible. Their visit at Christmas was approaching fast, and I looked forward to seeing them.

CHAPTER FIFTY-SEVEN

I was excited and a little nervous when both my son and daughter arranged their schedules so they could all come for Christmas with their families this year. They usually came in alternate years, but I felt the Lord was in this plan. In some ways, talking to them about the changes in me would be harder than offering my forgiveness to Dorjan. If he had been cold and nasty, as he was in Hungary, my life would have continued as usual. But if my children and their spouses reject me, I will be crushed, and the possibility of losing them is real.

I had to resolve this within myself before they came, or I would be robbed of my joy and peace. It was slipping away as fear tried to grip me, but peace was a treasure I was not willing to lose.

I have seen my family less often than I would have liked. Their busy lives are filled with sports and school events, so it is not easy for them to schedule a trip to visit 'Grandma'. With my pets and garden needing constant attention, my trips to the city were infrequent too. My family planned to stay until late on Boxing Day and drive the four hours home at night so the children could sleep during the trip.

The time had come to share my past with them, so I had copies of *My Early Years* for each of them. I had decided against posting it to them, as I wanted to talk about it in person.

They arrived with great excitement the day before Christmas Eve.

Michael and Katie arrived first with Caleb and Ruth. It has been several months since they have been here, and Caleb, now eight, and Ruth, who is six, have grown more than I had expected. We often talk on the phone, and so have been able to keep in close touch and hear the children's stories about school and their adventures, but being able to hug them and spend an extended time with them is always a delight.

Their chatter began as soon as their feet hit the ground.

'Grandma, we have brought lots of things to show you. I brought my new baby doll,' Ruth almost shouted, as I squeezed her, 'and a drawing of you that I did at school.'

Caleb endured a hug while asking, 'Where are Mango and Gypsy? Can I sit on Bessie while you milk her tomorrow?'

Amid the excitement, I saw Terry waving to me from her front yard. I waved back with a smile.

Michael asked, 'Isn't that Terror, and you are smiling and waving?'

I laughed and told him she was one of my closest friends now. I knew I had some explaining to do, and I was excited about it.

Michael is three years older than my daughter Rachael, but people assume Rachael is older. Not because she looks older than Michael, but because she has been the leader since she was about three, and Michael has not challenged the arrangement. He is more relaxed and easy-going than Rachael. People say he is more like me, and Rachael is like her dad.

Whereas Michael and Katie's arrival had been exciting but quiet, Rachael and Peter and their three children, Micah, Rebekah and Matthew, arrived in a whirlwind. They had driven an hour longer than Michael and Katie, but their arrival was filled with more noise and energy. Both parents looked exhausted. Micah is almost five, so a bit younger than Ruth. Rebekah is three, and Matthew is eighteen months old.

We took the children to the park to burn off the stored energy from sitting for hours in the cars. They love the park at

Wattle Creek, and the children all headed straight for the swings.

Katie, Rachael and I set up a picnic lunch on a table in the shade while the dads followed the children to the swings. We had a lazy lunch at the park, and when the younger children started to fade, we took them all home for naps.

I planned a barbecue in the backyard for dinner, followed by a quiet walk along the shore of the river, with all of us paddling our feet in the cool water.

The parents were tired from packing and travelling and went to bed early.

I enjoyed having the house full, with beds filled, and extra mattresses on the floor.

I sat up for a while, after everyone was in bed, praying and wondering what the Lord had planned for Christmas Eve.

CHAPTER FIFTY-EIGHT

About mid-afternoon on Christmas Eve, while we were sitting in the loungeroom eating fresh scones with jam and cream, Jason burst through the door in his usual manner, calling out, 'Grandma, where are you?'

My son and daughter gave me quizzical looks. I went to the door to greet him with a hug and a kiss. He had in his hand my Christmas present. I introduced him to my family, but he showed more interest in me opening my gift. He said he couldn't wait until Christmas Day to give it to me. I carefully opened it, with him beaming in front of me with his shoulders back and his chest puffed out. I removed from the package a long leather lead with a clasp on the end.

'I made it at school as Bessie needs a new lead. We can now throw away the old frayed rope we have been using.'

When I turned it over, I was extremely impressed with the stitching and how Jason had stamped BESSIE with leather lettering tools. He was very proud of what he had made, and I was very grateful. I thanked him, hugged him close and kissed his cheek again.

'It should be displayed on my wall, instead of staying out in the shed, as it was too beautiful to use.'

Then I pointed to a present under my tree and told him to open it. He commented excitedly on the weight. He guessed I had bought him a book, but when he opened it and read the title, 'The Australian Farmers Handbook', he was overjoyed. He took the shortcut through my back fence and ran to show 'Mr Jack'.

As soon as he left, my son turned to me, 'Grandma??' I

winked at him, saying, 'It is a long story. He is a boy who has been dealing with some difficulties in his life and needed a grandma.'

About half an hour later, I saw Jason climbing over my back fence again, but even from a distance, I saw tears. My heart sank. Had something happened to Jack?

When he came through my back door, he stammered, 'You won't believe it.'

It took him a while to catch his breath as he wiped his eyes.

'Mr Jack bought me a Merino ewe with three of the cutest lambs you could ever imagine.'

I sighed with relief.

Jason continued, 'He walked me to the shed, grinning so I felt a bit suspicious. I heard the bleating and raced in ahead of him. I told him how gorgeous the sweet lambs were when he put his arm around me, and while chuckling, said, 'Merry Christmas, Jason. They are yours.'

Jason said that was when the tears started. He hugged and hugged Mr Jack and could not find the words to thank him. He has never received such a gift. He said it felt like a dream.

Jack told Jason he wanted to teach him everything he knew about sheep. Together they planned over time to breed and buy others until they had a sizeable flock. Jack told Jason that he used to have over five hundred sheep, but he had trouble taking care of them all after his wife died. Jason was overwhelmed, with tears of joy running down his cheeks. Dear Jack.

Jason told me that when he showed Jack his book, he went straight into the house to his bookcase and pulled out his own dog-eared copy. He told Jason it was his favourite farming book and that he would learn a lot from reading it. That pleased me too.

Jason suggested that straight after Christmas, he take the grandchildren to Mr Jack's place to meet his lambs. He hadn't named them yet, so my grandchildren started thinking up names for his babies. He stayed and had a drink with us and devoured a few scones, while we all laughed and suggested some funny names. My son commented later on what a nice boy Jason was, and the others agreed. I felt very proud of him and delighted for both him and Jack.

Before Jason left, he turned to me, saying, 'I'm sorry, Grandma, if I scared you with my tears. I saw how worried you looked, but couldn't get the words out fast enough to tell you what had happened. You know I am a bit of a cry-baby...'

'No, Jason,' I assured him, 'You are not a cry-baby. Don't ever think or say that. As I have told you before, real men cry. It is a blessed thing to be able to express your joy as well as sadness. Repressed tears are too common, more so in men, and it is not always wise'. Smiling and squeezing his hand, I added, 'And tears of joy have a beauty of their own.'

CHAPTER FIFTY-NINE

That evening we ate barbecued sausages and salad outside, with the cicadas singing in the gum trees, with a cool breeze refreshing us after a hot day.

Dessert was my specialty - pavlova with bananas, passionfruit and my home-grown strawberries. Later, the children were tucked up in their beds after a day of swimming and playing by the river, and we five adults were sipping cool drinks on the back verandah overlooking the garden. Bessie kept a watchful eye on us as she contentedly chewed her cud.

In that moment of quiet, my son asked the one question I had been waiting for.

'So Mum, what has been going on?' And then he added with a chuckle, 'Or maybe I should say, who are you, and what have you done with our mother?'

His second question humbled me. I had hoped they could see a difference in me, but I hadn't expected the change to be so drastic. I thought back to the mother I had been to my children. Although they may think they had a very good childhood, my wounds and scars may have shown, although not in a way that children would understand. It was time to explain to them the missing pieces of my life.

I started by telling them about the book club and then how I found out a man I knew in Hungary now lived in Wattle Creek. I shocked them by saying that he had been the one person on earth I passionately hated and wanted to kill.

Rachael objected. 'Mum, you have always been sweet and kind to everyone. I can't imagine that you ever truly hated anyone.'

'It is time for me to share with you about my life before I came to Australia, things I have never told anyone before.'

I handed them each a copy of *My Early Years*, which included more details about my life than I had shared with the book club.

I busied myself cleaning up the dinner dishes while they all disappeared to various places around the house to read. Within an hour, we were all together in the loungeroom. In turn, they each hugged me, expressing their sympathy.

Michael took my hand, saying, 'Mum, I am deeply thankful to know what you have lived through. You and others who have suffered these things must get your stories out. We are all shocked and saddened, and I feel ashamed for not realising how the war affected you, and that I never even thought to ask.'

Rachael added, 'It is horrifying to read what happened to you and all the Jews, Mum, but I am interested to know why you left Hungary. Why didn't you choose to stay and rebuild your lives there? That must have been such a huge and painful decision. I think you and Grandma were extremely brave to come to Australia.'

'It wasn't easy, Rachael. You are right about that.

'The world outside of Europe was unknown to us, as we had never considered leaving Europe. Grandma spoke Hungarian and some Yiddish, and also German and Romanian, and could understand Serbian and French, but had no English. I had learned some English at school, but did not feel confident to speak it. I didn't have the gift of learning languages as fast as my mother.

'Grandma was frightened when we talked about moving to a Western, English-speaking country, but she knew it was the best choice.'

'I wish we could have had her with us longer and asked her questions.' Rachael said.

I smiled and said, 'Yes, I know you would have loved to hear her stories, but like me, she had tried to bury the past and neither of us spoke of it, not even to each other.

'Even though Hungary was free, things didn't change overnight. We had been outcasts for so long, we could not easily be convinced that we were now out of danger. We felt that things could change in a moment, and we could be the hunted ones again. When the fear gets deep inside, it does not easily disappear. Our eyes could see some changes, but it would take a long time for our hearts to believe it.

'We found the majority of our extended family and friends had not survived, and our house had been destroyed. Everyone changed after what we had been through. Those who had endured labour camps and concentration camps were hardly recognisable.'

'It is unbelievable that people could be that cruel to fellow human beings,' Katie muttered.

'Yes, it is, Katie. Some people today can't believe it happened, and there are even those who are trying to erase it from the history books.

'The condition of the survivors of the concentration and labour camps broke our hearts. I can still see their faces. Most of those who had survived were no longer the same people mentally. Now there is a term for it - Post Traumatic Stress Syndrome. After the war, no term existed for such a condition, and no treatment. The worst-affected people were like shadows.

'Mum and I were among the lucky ones who had escaped that nightmare. No one could return to pre-war life. We were trying to live in a broken country filled with broken people.'

Peter said, 'Yes, it's crazy. The whole of Europe was affected. Hundreds of thousands of innocent lives destroyed, and not just those killed.'

I continued. 'The fear didn't leave us overnight, and we had lost almost all of our possessions. We tried to find the people who were looking after our gold and jewellery, but some of those people were missing.

'Also, our fellow Hungarians had been brainwashed through

posters, newspapers and books, so anti-Semitism did not disappear overnight, and even still exists today.

'Like thousands of others, we decided to leave Europe, feeling it would be the only possible way to experience real freedom.'

Peter asked, 'So, how did you decide where to go? That must have been a tough decision.'

'There were limited choices, Peter. Only a few countries accepted Hungarian refugees. We decided to go to Great Britain, but it was not easy. Being Hungarian and Jewish still had disadvantages after the war. We managed to travel to Germany, but we were 'D.P.s' or 'Displaced Persons'. To get a visa, we needed passports, and getting passports was a problem. However, the British Consulate in Frankfurt could issue us passports, although they were Stateless ones.

'In my letter, I explained how we came from Britain to Australia on the assisted passage scheme.'

Rachael remarked, 'But there are parts of the story missing, Mum. Have you driven Dorjan out of town? I don't think you murdered him, as you had planned, and I can't see any hint of hatred in you now.'

Michael added, 'And you don't even hate Terry anymore. I haven't heard you grumble about her once since we have been here. I even saw you smile and wave. This is the story that I am interested in hearing.'

So, I silently prayed and began.

I shared with them my reaction to learning Dorjan had moved here. Rachael, who is forthright, unlike her mother, determined she would have gone straight to the supermarket and abused him loudly for all to hear. I'm glad she wasn't visiting then and that I hadn't told her about it at the time. She may have rushed to Wattle Creek and caused all sorts of trouble in a valiant effort to execute justice for her mother.

'So, what did you do, Mum?' Katie asked.

I explained how and why I hid away and told them how

Aunty Julia had rescued me.

They were all indignant when they heard about the yellow cardboard stars. I confessed how I assumed Terry made them, and with embarrassment, detailed the shameful things I had said and done. They were proud of me for confronting her, as they knew Terry and I had an unpleasant history.

'But,' I said, 'it wasn't Terry.'

My daughter was convinced that wicked Mr Halmi was behind it.

I recounted Terry's role and filled them in on my discovery of the culprit. They all hoped I had made him pay handsomely for being so cruel. They assumed I reported him to the police, but I said I had not.

I would have enjoyed telling them about Jason, but it was his story to tell if he ever wanted to, not mine.

I then came to the story of Terry and told them about my remorse. But they wanted to know if Terry had somehow changed and why she was being kind. I said I had invited her for Christmas lunch after church, and she could tell them her story.

'After church ???', they exclaimed in unison.

CHAPTER SIXTY

As expected, the children were up before the sun with their eyes trained on the coloured parcels under the Christmas tree. We had a special time exchanging gifts and enjoyed our traditional Christmas breakfast of toast, Vegemite and bunches of local cherries, while the Christmas pudding simmered on the stove. Due to the hot weather, we traditionally cook the turkey the day before and have it cold on Christmas Day with a variety of salads. We always have hot Christmas pudding for dessert, no matter how hot the day. We eat it with generous amounts of Bessie's cream and scoops of custard and ice cream. This is something special we eat only at Christmas, and we all look forward to it.

The subject of church came up again during breakfast. I said I would be going, and they could come if they wanted to. They all agreed to come, mainly because they were curious about what I had joined, and Rachael wanted to make sure that I had not joined a cult. Neither of my children nor their spouses had ever been inside a church. I would have forbidden my children to go when they were young if they had asked.

Shortly before 10 am, we all walked into the church. Heads turned as people saw my family arrive with me, and my friends gave them warm smiles. We found enough space for us all about halfway down on the right-hand side, so we all shuffled into the row and sat together.

The children were looking around and taking in all the unfamiliar sights and sounds. They enjoyed watching the musicians getting ready to play. The music started soon after we were seated, and we stood to sing. My family followed along well, with the words on the overhead projector screen. Even the children were enjoying the songs. I was praying for them all, and my friends possibly were also. The songs we sang were as unfamiliar to them as they had been to me. The words may have been raising questions in their minds. 'My Redeemer Lives' and 'Oh the Blood of Jesus' were songs the Lord had maybe chosen today, especially for my family.

I knew they were somewhat familiar with parts of the Christmas story because Christmas carols were played in all the supermarkets and shops during the Christmas season. We sang, 'Oh come all ye Faithful', and 'Oh Holy Night'. After the singing, David came onto the stage and asked all the children to come and sit down at the front. My grandchildren didn't need any encouragement to slip out of their seats and hurry down. I enjoyed seeing them so comfortable in this unfamiliar environment. David said he would tell us the true story of Christmas. With the use of the overhead projector, he asked the children to choose which Christmas card told the real story of what happened at Christmas. The first picture had some shepherds, 3 'wise men', Mary, Joseph and Jesus all together in a stable, surrounded by sheep and cattle. I picked that one as it looked right to me. The following one had the shepherds with Jesus and Mary with a star shining in the sky over them. The third one had three wise men, Mary, Joseph and baby Jesus. Almost all the children chose the first picture, so I felt confident now that I was right. He then asked the congregation to choose. Several adults also chose the first one. I had read the story, but I was a bit hazy on the details. He then said he had tricked us, as none of the pictures were correct. Now he had our attention. I felt sure the Christmas cards that we bought would be correct.

He read to us from Luke 2 about some shepherds who, while watching their sheep one night, suddenly saw a huge angel standing in front of them. He told them not to be afraid and announced that the Saviour of the world had that night been born. Then the sky filled with angels praising God. David mentioned that we don't know how long the angels filled the sky, but after they disappeared, the shepherds went to Bethlehem, about an eight or nine-kilometre walk, where the angel had said Jesus had been born. They found Mary and Joseph, and the baby, possibly on the ground floor of Joseph's relative's house, where the animals were kept in the winter. Since it was not winter, no animals would be in there, so it would have been nice and clean and private. The Bible says all the guest rooms in the house were full, but they needed a quiet place to have the baby, so that would have been a perfect place. He said we don't have all the details, but because of the culture of the time, and the fact that they were in Bethlehem with all of Joseph's extended family, we can be sure Mary would have been well cared for during the birth of her baby.

The idea that Jesus was born in a stable in the middle of a field with just Joseph and some animals does not fit with the culture or the lifestyle of the time in which Jesus was born.

David asked the children, 'When did the wise men come?'

A boy answered, 'The next day?' David praised him for a good guess but said he wasn't quite correct. Then he asked them, 'How many wise men were there?' In unison, the children called out, 'Three.'

David laughed, clapped and said, 'You are all wrong. But I know you think that because they brought three types of gifts. Can you remember what they were?' One child called out, 'Gold, Frankenstein and myrrh.'

The congregation chuckled.

'Very close, Joshy. You almost got them all right', David said with a smile, not wanting to embarrass the small boy.

'Now I will tell you what happened. We must find out what the Bible says, rather than getting our information from songs or Christmas cards.'

He read the story of the Magi coming to see Jesus. Then he told us that there were some clues in that story about the number of wise men who came, and when they came. He read how all of Jerusalem was amazed at their arrival.

'Would everyone be amazed if three strangers came into our town?' he asked. 'No, of course not. And Bethlehem was a lot bigger than Wattle Creek.'

He said historians, who know about magi of that time, say there could have been even one hundred of them for all of Jerusalem to be aware of their arrival. Then David asked us when we thought they arrived. I wondered about this, as I assumed they were there with the shepherds. David explained how wicked Herod was upset by the magi's words about a king being born. He felt threatened by a baby. The magi left town after seeing Jesus, without telling Herod where to find Him.

'Herod was angry that they didn't tell him where the young king was located, and as a result he had all the boys in and around Bethlehem under the age of two killed. Why that age? Because Herod estimated that Jesus would have been a bit younger than 2, maybe 18 months old or so. That means the magi were there, not when Jesus was newly born, but when he was a toddler. They had travelled a great distance to see Jesus.'

David then read the whole section about Joseph being told in a dream to go to Egypt just before Herod killed the boys, and they packed up and left in the middle of the night. David then emphasised to all of us to be careful to get our information from the Word of God and no other source. He emphasised that this is critical for learning about Jesus, and what He did and taught. There is a vast amount of false teaching in the churches, and we can recognise what is true if we know what the Bible says. He then talked about Jesus' ministry, His death and resurrection. He spoke about the return of Jesus, which is still in the future, explaining that at Christmas we remember mainly Jesus's birth. However, the details of His life, death, resurrection and return all need to be studied. He finished by explaining about Jesus' return and highlighted some of the signs that it is getting closer.

At the end of the service, we all stood to sing two songs: 'Thine Be the Glory', a song about Jesus's victory over the devil by

His resurrection, and 'Joy to the World', a Christmas carol, which is a song about His triumphant return, which we eagerly await.

When the service finished, we filed out of the church. Friends wanted to be introduced to the family, so it took a while to get to the door. David and Karen were keen to meet them and mentioned that they were looking forward to seeing them at the Boxing Day picnic.

As we headed towards the door, Brenda took me aside. Looking worried, she said, 'Louisa, I have been wanting to tell you something. I got some bad news yesterday. That coffee shop chain, Kaffeine Kingdom, is planning to come to Wattle Creek. It will be the end of Common Ground, Louisa.'

'Can we stop them, Brenda?'

With a deep sigh, she said, 'I don't know. I honestly don't know.'

Brenda brushed most challenges off with a joke and a laugh, but not this.

I hugged her and assured her that we would all do whatever we could to stop this from happening.

'Come and have lunch with us, Brenda.'

'Thanks, Louisa, but I am spending the day with Charlotte and the children. My car is loaded with gifts and food!'

She smiled weakly and was then distracted by a loud, 'Merry Christmas, Brenda,' and a hug from one of her loyal customers.

I had forgotten to tell the family about the picnic, so when we arrived home from church, I filled them in on the plan. They were interested to meet the rest of the book club, and my family always enjoys a picnic.

We had no time to sit and chat when we reached home, as we had a feast to prepare. After a quick cup of tea, we started work in the kitchen while the children played outside with Gypsy.

CHAPTER SIXTY-ONE

We had lunch prepared when Jack and Terry arrived. I had invited Jack as I heard he would be alone for Christmas. Terry spent a considerable amount of time with Jack since she had started cleaning for him, and I enjoyed watching their friendship deepen.

Jack had attended church for the first time this Christmas.

We set the children up with a table on the back verandah while we adults ate in my dining room. With plates full of cold turkey and salads, the conversation started, and my daughter leapt straight in.

'So, Terry. Mum says you have experienced some significant changes in your life. Could you tell us what has happened, or am I being rude to ask?'

Terry beamed as she said she loved talking about the things God has done. Rachael turned to me, and hiding her face from the others, rolled her eyes, smiled and winked.

Terry told them what she had shared with me weeks earlier about her childhood and how and why she had avoided relationships. She had chosen instead to be cold and rude to drive people away and prevent further hurt. She said how Karen had insisted on getting behind her wall and, leaning forward and touching my arm, told them how sorry she felt for how she had treated me in the past. She explained better than I could have what Jesus has done for us all. She talked about His sacrifice, which they had heard about in church that morning, and the response that He requires from us. She shared how Jesus had healed her heart and forgiven her for all the things she had ever said and done.

She described her baptism and how clean and forgiven she felt, like a rebirth, a fresh start, and how the anger and bitterness had gone.

My children were relaxed through this conversation, but Michael's wife, Katie, seemed uncomfortable. Peter and Rachael asked Terry some thoughtful questions, but Katie remained silent, staring at her food. Michael asked Terry how she could be certain it was all true.

She smiled and answered, 'Once I was lost, now I am found. Nothing and no one could have healed me and changed me the way Jesus has. The more I know Him, the more I love Him.'

My son-in-law, Peter, then turned to me, saying, 'So Mum, do you have a similar story? I have never heard anything like this before. I have not known Terry well, except for your complaints in the past,' he added with a cheeky grin and a wink in Terry's direction. Terry threw her head back laughing.

'But, Mum, I can see a change in you that I can't explain. I must admit I am still angry about Dorjan and what he did to you and your family, but I can see that you are not.'

I smiled. 'Did you see that man who came and put his arm around my shoulder and said 'Merry Christmas' as we were leaving church this morning?'

They thought for a moment and all nodded, and Rachael said, 'Yes, he seemed like a sweet man.'

'That was Dorjan.'

Mouths fell open, eyes wide.

I turned to Peter, saying that yes, my story is similar. As we devoured oversized helpings of Christmas pudding, I told them that when I saw Terry remove the yellow stars, I realised I was the nasty neighbour with the hard heart. Terry kept her eyes on her pudding while I spoke. I shared how helpless and hopeless I had felt and how I had called Karen. I went into detail about my talks with Karen and Terry and told them about my baptism and how clean and renewed I felt. I smiled at Terry as I explained that I could forgive Terry and even Mr Halmi because of the forgiveness I received.

Jack listened intently and said Terry had told him her story, and he was grateful to hear mine.

He added, 'I have a lot to process. I have asked Terry questions over the last months, and I am spending a lot of time thinking about these things. I have been asking Jason questions too, and some he can answer, and some set him thinking too.'

I could feel the Holy Spirit working in some hearts as we ate together.

After lunch, we headed to the creek so the children and their parents could cool off. We oldies sat on the bank with our feet dangling in the cool water. Despite the heat which is common at Christmas, a breeze made the day pleasant. We spent a relaxing time watching the antics of the younger members of my family and enjoying each other's company. This Christmas Day was a long way removed from anything I had experienced before.

At our last book club meeting, we planned a picnic together on Boxing Day, the day after Christmas, at the beautiful park in the centre of town. I was glad my family would be meeting my friends, and also meet some of my friends' extended families. We were going to be quite a crowd.

CHAPTER SIXTY-TWO

I had asked Jason to milk Bessie the next morning, as I would be busy organising breakfast and preparing lunch for the picnic. He hoisted 8-year-old Caleb onto her back, and as Jason milked, Caleb chatted nonstop.

After joining us for breakfast, Jason took the children to meet his lambs, and they rushed back chatting excitedly, describing each lamb to their parents. The names the children thought were perfect for the lambs were cute, but 'Fluffy', 'Skippy' and 'Snowy' were names that definitely wouldn't last.

Every town in Australia has a beautiful public park near its centre, and Wattle Creek is no exception. We had planned to arrive at about eleven o'clock, so there would be time for games and activities before we ate our lunch. The fresh mown grass invited us to spread our blankets and relax, as the children headed straight to the swings and slides.

The traditional game of cricket was soon underway. The sound of bat on ball, the shouts and cheers of the players, mingled with the laughter of children and the songs of the birds, made our picnic complete.

We invited Jack as we had made him an honorary member of the club, and he was delighted to join in the game of cricket. He is fit and healthy now, having experienced a physical recovery and a renewed zest for life. Seeing him showing off his cricket skills and impressing the younger players with his prowess and stamina was a joy to watch.

As all the activity stimulated appetites, the time came to spread out our bountiful assortment of Christmas Day leftovers.

The park's picnic tables were wisely placed beneath its aged Moreton Bay Fig trees, with their swaying branches fanning away the heat of the summer day.

The girls and I made salad and turkey sandwiches, wrapped up some cold Christmas pudding, and brought some Christmas treats to share that none of us could face the day before after too much pudding. Everyone came with chicken, turkey and ham left from the previous day, and slices, cakes and other treats. We settled in for another day of feasting.

During the afternoon, I noticed Marianne and Alan deep in conversation with Peter and Michael. Alan wasn't interested in small talk and soon led them into a meaningful discussion. It encouraged me to see they were thinking seriously about what they had heard and seen over the last couple of days.

I felt concerned about Katie as she had been quiet since church, and looked uncomfortable at Christmas Day lunch. She concentrated on her children and kept herself out of the deeper discussions.

I had the opportunity to chat with Michael, who, aware of her struggle, encouraged me not to worry. He said she takes time to process new things, and together they would talk through what they had heard. I wondered if something deeper might be disturbing her.

Rachael chatted with Terry and shared our sandwiches. I prayed that Terry would help Rachael understand the news about Jesus. It seemed to be where their conversation was heading, so I moved away. Rachael would not be shy with her comments and questions.

Brenda brought a man with her from a nearby town, and we were curious to meet him. She told us they had a mutual friend and met a few times over the last couple of years. Recently, they had started to correspond regularly, and when Brenda had told him about the fair and our float, he had come to see it. Since then, Brenda and Ian, a solicitor, have spent more time together.

The threat of the coffee shop chain seemed to be mercifully

forgotten for now.

I hadn't had an opportunity to get to know Joanna, so I spent some time with her and her family. Her two sons were delightful young men who both work in Sydney and came for Christmas with their wives and children. I had never seen Joanna this animated, as she relished every moment with her boys and their families.

Joanna's mother may join us at the book club occasionally, although she is a little deaf and no longer fluent in English. Joanna had been touched by the love shown to her mother when we cleaned Jack's house, so she felt sure she would feel comfortable at the book club, even if she didn't follow all the discussion.

Irene came with Malcolm and, instead of joining the game of cricket, which she previously would have done, sat holding hands with him while chatting with David and Karen. Irene had told me both David and Alan have been spending time with Malcolm, and life is again peaceful at home. Malcolm seemed relaxed and attentive to Irene. She caught me watching her and smiled.

I hadn't seen Julia often over the last few weeks, as we had both been busy preparing for the Christmas holidays. Everyone laughed when she shared how our book club decided to do what we could to help sick or shut-in people in our town, after our experience with Jack. She told them how five of us knocked on a door with a delicious-smelling casserole, flowers and a cake, plus mops, buckets and cleaning supplies, and discovered that we were at the wrong house. We left a confused young man at the door as we mumbled our apologies and made our retreat.

Karen and David came with their two skilled cricket players and a lady, Sue, who had recently moved to our town and had expressed interest in joining the book club. She had a son about Jason's age who wore a scowl and wasn't interested in talking to anyone. Jason invited him to join the cricket game, but after receiving a rude reply, Jason walked away.

The picnic too quickly drew to a close as the shadows lengthened, and my family planned to start their trip home soon after dark.

Before we packed up to leave, Rachael took my arm and asked me to walk with her. She said she loved to see me so content, and thought the book club was perhaps the best thing that had happened to me in recent years. She could see that we were a close-knit group and had heard stories of our adventures together.

She added, 'Mum, I know that is not the only thing, or even the most important thing that's happened to you. You are now a different, peaceful person, and your eyes seem to shine with new life. When we were young, you were pleased that Michael and I were not interested in religion, and you avoided any talk about being Jewish. Now I see all that has changed. 'So Mum, while we walk,' she added, 'could you please tell me more about Jesus?

The End

EPILOGUE

Towards the end of January, I took a short trip to Sydney to see my children and grandchildren. On my way home, when I reached Wattle Creek, I stopped first at the cafe to tell Brenda all my exciting news.

She gave me a warm welcome home and made me a cup of my favourite tea. The news poured out of me.

'Brenda, they are all saved and baptised! You won't believe how it happened. Michael told me he and Katie had bought a Bible and together they had searched the Scriptures to see if what they had heard over Christmas was true. They both gave their lives to the Lord and joined a house church, which one of Michael's workers belongs to. Katie explained to me that she had trouble seeing God as loving because she had grown up with an unkind father. However, when she read how Jesus was the exact representation of the heavenly Father and saw His amazing love, she turned her heart towards her eternal Father.

'The sweetest thing was that they waited to get baptised until I could be there to witness it!

'But here is another beautiful part of the story, Brenda. Rachael and Peter had been full of questions since Christmas too, and they came to watch Michael and Katie get baptised. Some people talked to them over lunch, answering many questions, and to my amazement, they borrowed some old clothes and also were baptised! As so often happens, the Lord did more than we dared to ask for or imagine. Brenda, when I saw Rachael walk into the water, it was as if sunshine had suddenly burst through the clouds!'

Brenda smiled as I shared the marvellous news, but she wasn't her normal enthusiastic self.

'Brenda, what's wrong?'
She heaved a big sigh that seemed to have travelled up from her toes.

'Louisa, it is so good to have you home. I am worried. Do you remember at Christmas I told you about Kaffeine Kingdom's plans to invade Wattle Creek and set up one of their awful coffee shops? Well, it looks like it is going to happen. I don't think there is any way we can stop them. This will be the end of my coffee shop and mean the eventual disappearance of small family-owned businesses here. Our beloved town will never be the same. I have seen this happen in other towns. We won't survive.'

AFTERWORD

Dear readers, thank you for your interest in Louisa and the many characters and dramas in the little town of Wattle Creek. If you send your email address to me at alisonmiles@protonmail.com I will be happy to let you know when you can read Book Two, and find out how Brenda copes with the "Kaffeine Kingdom" invasion, and other adventures and challenges affecting her and the other lovely ladies in the Book Club in Wattle Creek and the people of that beautiful town.

ABOUT THE AUTHOR

Alison Miles

Alison Miles is an Australian mother of seven and grandmother of twenty. Together with her husband, she has had the joy and challenge of homeschooling all their children. Over the years, she has lived in Australia, the United States, and currently she and her husband live in Malaysia.

The most important thing in her life is to serve the Lord with all her heart and to walk in daily obedience to Him.

BOOKS BY THIS AUTHOR

Group Bible Study

You think you don't know the Bible well enough? No problem
You feel you lack the skills to make it exciting so people want to keep coming? We've got you covered.
Click the link below and grab this easy to read practical guide, and you are on your way to an exciting and fruitful adventure.
It is easier than you think and possibly more rewarding than you have imagined.
So let's get started!

Thinking Of Home Schooling?

This book is for those considering taking the first step in educating their children at home, but who have many questions about how to start and how to be successful. It will equip you with helpful information which will build your confidence and help get you started.

www.ingramcontent.com/pod-product-compliance
Lightning Source LLC
LaVergne TN
LVHW100526110826
845146LV00002B/791

* 9 7 9 8 2 1 8 9 2 0 9 5 1 *